—law ess—
deception

THE RETRIBUTION DUET
BOOK ONE

IMOGEN WELLS

Foreword

This book contains scenes and themes that some readers may find upsetting and/or offensive. Scenes of explicit sex, violence and profanity can be found in the pages that follow.
This is book one of two and ends on a cliffhanger.

The author is British, and British English spellings and phrases are used throughout. If there are any words or phrases that you are unsure of, please do not hesitate to contact me.
Imogenwells.author@gmail.com

Prologue

Roxy

I stroll back to my car, muttering and cursing. Jumping in, I head towards the station and pull into the carpark just as a call comes through on the radio. With nothing better to do while I wait, I tell dispatch that I'll check it out. As I'm spinning the car round, my phone rings.

"Whitmore," I snap, feeling ever so slightly tetchy.

"I've got that location you asked for," comes a voice down the line.

"Grand. Send it to me." I don't bother with any other niceties or a goodbye. I drive to the warehouse, and my phone pings with a message just as I turn into the carpark.

When I pull up to the warehouse, there's no sign of anyone and the alarm has stopped ringing. I quickly check the message with Jess' location and knowing exactly where she is, I have a quick look around just to be sure. After a walk by of the whole building and no sign of anything suspicious, I turn back towards my car.

Suddenly, the car park is lit up as headlights switch on from somewhere to the left of me. I can't see jack shit with

1

them glaring in my face. It's probably the keyholder for the warehouse having been alerted of the triggered alarm.

"You mind turning your damn lights off, buddy," I yell across the carpark as I move forward, trying to step out of the light.

The squeak of car doors opening and then slamming shut reaches me, and I reach for my phone.

"I wouldn't do that if I were you," a voice rumbles back to me at the same time as the snick of a gun echoes.

A feeling of disbelief and shock and something else, which I can't quite name, shivers down my spine at the sound of the voice.

It's a voice I recognise, but one I've not heard in almost eleven years.

Just as I'm wondering if he's here too and at what point my mouth will form some fucking words to find out, the deep baritone that used to make me weak at the knees and light up my fucking world, booms out over the empty space.

"Long time no see, Roxanne." The sound of my name on his lips and the way he rolls the R are like a song you haven't heard in an age but know every word, every little cadence to. It's almost enough to eclipse the shock and quickly building anger but not quite.

"Fuck you, Maddox." I begin walking to my car, my phone vibrating in my pocket, only to be halted as a gunshot rings out, and the bullet narrowly misses my foot, kicking up dust from the ground. I spin on my heels and march towards them.

"What the fuck is wrong with you, huh?" Another shot, again just missing my feet. I don't stop. "You going to fucking shoot me, Maddox?" There are no more shots, as I knew there wouldn't be. If he wanted me dead, I'd be six feet under already.

Stepping past the beam of the headlights, I get a clear view of two of the most well-known brothers in London. Notorious for their ruthlessness and ability to demand respect, even from those above them in the underworld.

Maddox and Zachary Lawler.

I knew this day would come. I've been waiting for it.

But I was not prepared for the two men that now stand in front of me.

Two men that threaten everything I've built.

The only men that have the power to unravel me.

"Not going to shoot you, Roxanne, just making sure we have your full attention." Shoving down my shock at seeing them and the raging river of emotions rushing through me, I take another step forward, turning my undivided attention to Maddox.

"Well, you've got it, so what the fuck can I do for you, do tell?"

"It's more of a what we can do for you."

From the corner of my eye, I watch as Zak places the gun in a holster inside his suit jacket before stepping around the car and stopping next to Maddox.

"There's nothing you can possible do for me, other than continue to leave me the fuck alone. And I need to be somewhere." I turn from them and begin walking back towards my car.

"We have some information about your mum, Roxanne." I stop dead, but I don't turn around, and Maddox continues, "We need your help, and in return we will tell you what we know."

"No thanks." I'm desperate for answers but not that desperate.

"You have two weeks, Roxanne. Two weeks to decide what's more important, your job or getting those elusive answers."

Now I spin around. "You're blackmailing me? Ten years of nothing, and then you turn up to fucking blackmail me." I let out a disbelieving laugh. "This would be good if you had anything on me. So again, thanks but no thanks."

"We have plenty, but who says you need hard evidence. The rumour mill is a wonderous thing, and in your circle, I imagine it can destroy a career in the blink of an eye. Two weeks, Roxanne. We'll be in touch." And with that, they climb back into their car and peel out of here, leaving me standing in a dark, empty car park and wondering what the fuck just happened.

Chapter One

Roxy

I'm bone tired and stressed to high heaven. You wouldn't think I just spent the last two weeks doing nothing but making a nuisance of myself in the most beautiful location. I've been a major cock-block to my best friend Jess and her brash arsehole of a fiancé. Despite the fact he's an arsehole, he's the best kind, and I couldn't be happier for her.

I've also just made the biggest bust in the history of human trafficking. One that has lit a fuse beneath the government, police and courts.

I haul the bag onto my shoulder as I head to my front door, tensing as my phone pings again. It's been blowing up since I switched it back on an hour ago.

Two weeks. That's all I got to make a decision that could change the course of my life. A decision that will have devastating consequences no matter what I decide.

My whole life has been one walked on the very edge of right and wrong. Mostly wrong when I was younger. It's not a surprise when your mother was a junkie and the man who so kindly knocked her up is now the head of the judiciary and president of the courts in England and Wales.

I dump my bag on the floor in the hall and make straight for the kettle. A shot of caffeine and some toast are at the top of my list right now, closely followed by a steaming hot shower.

I fill the kettle, and while I wait for it to boil, I find the bread and milk I just bought from the shop. Shoving two slices in the toaster, I stand and tap my fingers against the counter.

I'm just pouring the water into my cup when the doorbell rings.

"Fuck's sake!"

As I reach the door, I peek through the spyhole and see it's Mrs Downs from next door. She's the Dot Cotton of the road. The nosy neighbour who sees and hears everything. Of course, she heads up the neighbourhood watch scheme too.

Swinging the door open, I greet her with a painted-on smile.

"Mrs Downs, how lovely to see you. What can I do for you?" I use my telephone voice. You know the one we all have when we want to appear professional and well mannered.

"Miss Whitmore, you're back I see."

"So it seems."

"Yes, well, I thought I saw you arriving and wanted to let you know immediately about some rather unsavoury characters that were hanging around outside your house this past week."

"Is that right. And who might these..." I wait for her to fill in the gaps as I know she will. The woman simply can't help herself. It's like a compulsion to stick her nose in and gossip endlessly.

"Well, two men you see. They came by every evening. Only they didn't stay long. Just seemed to knock, look around and then leave again. I know that in your line of work you must interact with some questionable members of society, although I've never seen them at your house before, so I thought it best to let you know. One of them at least had a suit on, but he had tattoos and a piercing in his eyebrow. The other, well, he was kind of angry looking. Tall and broad with a dark head of hair. So vastly different from one another. I found it quite strange, you know." She trails off, almost wistfully.

Before I can even think to reply, the fire alarm blares from the kitchen, and the smell of burnt toast wafts down the hall to me.

"Shit!" I race away from the door, leaving it ajar. Wisps of smoke plume from the toaster, and as I reach it, I flip the switch. The charred remains of my toast pop up. "Fuck my life every which way!"

A small gasp from behind me has me twisting to see Mrs Downs standing with her hand covering her mouth. And it's not because of the amount of smoke that's filled the room.

"Thanks for letting me know, Mrs Downs," I say, ushering her back towards the front door. "But as you can see, I have a mess to clean up, so if you don't mind." I hold the front door open, almost slamming it shut before she can turn around, but I refrain.

"Oh, well, yes...I'll see you later," she stutters and hurries back down the path.

I close the door and rush to open the kitchen window, which looks out over my back garden. It's not much, but in London having any sort of garden is a luxury.

My phone continues to buzz non-stop while I drink my tea and clear up, but I ignore it. I'm holding on to the last few hours before I need to make my final decision. And I know if I don't, it will be made for me.

I'm not usually an indecisive person. In fact, I've been accused many a time of making hasty decisions in the heat of the moment. Even so, they've always been well thought out.

I follow my gut. Being a cop means good instincts are a must, and I follow mine always.

This time, my gut says that either choice is a bad one.

Dumping my cup in the sink, I grab my phone. Trying to avoid looking at all the messages and missed calls, I quickly find Jess' number and send her a text to say I'm home safe before hauling my shit upstairs and take a shower.

By the time I reach the station my mood hasn't improved, and as if to throw another coal onto the burning fire that is my life, my phone pings with another countdown message. An hourly reminder that in four hours my life will implode no matter what my decision.

I push through the station doors and am met with a symphony of sounds, all of which make my head hurt and emphasise everything I've worked my arse off for and will lose by the end of all this. I shake away the thoughts as someone calls out to me.

"Hey, Sarge, good to have you back. Did you miss me?"

"Sure, I did, Smithy," I say all saccharine sweet, patting his cheek as I reach him. I wait for the first hint of a smile before continuing, "About as much as I miss a case of the clap." Several of the guys closest to us begin to laugh as I walk away, and I can hear them ribbing him mercilessly. It's all in good humour. Smithy is a good guy and decent cop. We've worked a couple of cases before, and he has a way with words that builds an easy rapport with people, both victims and suspects. I'd rather have him at my back over some of the other arseholes that work here.

I drop down into my chair and stare at the mountain of paperwork sitting on my desk. Taking the top file, I see it's a case review for a missing person from two years ago. Only now it seems like there's been a development. Most likely a result of the recent trafficking ring bust. As I go through more of the files, I realise they are all linked in some way to trafficking.

"Welcome back, Whitmore," I mutter to myself as I open the file on a murder case from a month ago. This one I remember vividly. Hard to forget finding a dead body with their head missing, and as if that wasn't enough, when we did discover the head, it was in bed next to the victim's wife. It might not have been a horse's head, but the message was clear all the same: You're dead.

My life is one long death filled drama show, and it's not about to improve any.

Chapter Two

Maddox

A low moan fills the room, and I swear there's a hint of pain there too, but I don't stop. Pulling back, I slam forward as my balls draw up tight, and the bitch I'm buried inside screams out in pleasure or pain, I don't give a fuck. Tightening my grip on her nape, I pound into her again and again until the familiar feeling of release rushes over me.

The relief it brings is short lived, and I pull out as quick as I entered her. Releasing her, I dispose of the condom and am just tucking my cock back inside my boxers as the door flies open and in storms Zak.

"That fucking little weasel Tommy. I'm—ah, fuck, man," he groans, covering his eyes before turning around.

Heather yanks her skirt back down over her arse as she rises from her position bent over my desk. She takes a couple of hesitant steps forward, wobbly on her feet from the fucking she just received. When she reaches me and stretches out a hand to my chest, I snatch her wrist away.

"Hands to yourself, bitch. Now, get the fuck out of here." Letting her hand go, she glares at me before turning and stomping away. The slamming of my office door is her final *fuck you*, but it's barely a blip on my conscience.

"What's Tommy done now?" I ask, rounding my desk and sitting down. When Zak doesn't answer, I raise my head to see him staring at me. "What the fuck's your problem?"

"That," he says, nodding towards the closed door and referring to the chick I was just fucking. "Heather, of all the girls here, you choose her. She's nasty, man." His lips turn up in disgust.

"Fuck you, Zak. When you're pissed you pump iron, me, I like to pump pussy. So fucking what."

"Okay, man, your funeral. But there's a hint of desperation wafting amongst the sex scented cloud above your fucking head."

My eyes narrow at him, and he lets out a deep laugh. "Get to the fucking point of you barging into my office."

Zak's laughter is quickly replaced with a scowl. "The fucker tipped off Rogers. When we arrived, the cunt had already gone."

"You're sure?"

"No, I'm not fucking sure, but who else would be stupid enough?"

"And let me guess, no sign of Tommy anywhere, right?" Zak nods, pulling his phone from his pocket as it pings. He's not telling me anything I don't already know. I'm expecting a visitor who might be able to shed some light on where Tommy is. I watch as a gratified smile kicks up the corner of Zak's mouth, and his pierced eyebrow rises with it.

"What you grinning about?"

"Oh, you know, just tormenting a certain Detective Sergeant with some hourly reminders."

"She said anything yet?" I ask, reaching for a cigarette and lighting it up. The smoke plumes above me as I exhale, and I'm reminded of a time when things were simpler.

"Not even a fuck you for the last few hours."

I take another drag of my cigarette, inhaling deeply, letting the smoke infect my lungs. I can almost feel the black tar as it encases them, shortening my life with every breath. But it won't be what ends me. No, my death will come by the hands of another, and I'll almost be grateful for it.

"You think she's going to do it?" Zak asks, twisting the bar in his eyebrow. It's his tell that he's nervous. One only I and maybe one other person knows about.

"She doesn't have a lot of fucking choice, Zak." His hand drops from his piercing, and he looks right at me.

"No, she doesn't, but this is Rox, man. We both know she won't like being backed into a corner. She'll come out fighting. Spitting venom with every hit, every word."

"Don't you think I know that, but what else do you want me to do, huh? Besides, she hates us anyway, so what harm is a little more going to do," I say with a shrug.

"That what you tell yourself when you're sticking your dick in all those bitches?"

"Fuck. You! Fucking hypocrite," I snap back.

There's a sharp rap of knuckles on the door before it opens and Ripley walks in.

"He's here, boss."

"Good fucking timing." I discard the rest of my fag in the ashtray and follow Ripley downstairs.

It's still early and only a few tables are occupied. Candi is entertaining a couple of old suits on the far stage, and Lila is serving a man who could be eating and drinking through a straw for next six months if he doesn't have the answers I want.

Lila's eyes flick to me, then quickly behind me to where Zak is before focusing back on the man in front of her. She doesn't say anything, doesn't give away that we are right behind him.

I slap my hand down on his back just as he takes a sip of his drink, causing him to spit it out all over the bar.

"Sammy, Sammy, Sammy," I taunt, gripping the back of his neck. Lila places an Old Fashioned on the bar in front of me and a straight up shot of Macallan on the rocks for Zak. I give a nod of thanks before she walks back down the bar to serve someone else.

I pick up my drink, taking a mouthful and tightening my grip on Sammy's neck when he tries to look my way.

I bend down close to his ear. "Where the fuck is your brother?"

A girly squeak escapes at the sound of my voice before he tries to stutter out a reply. "C-c-come on, Maddox, we're friends, right."

"We're not fucking friends, Sammy," I bite out, slamming his head into the bar. There's a loud crack quickly punctuated by a gurgled cry of pain. When I yank his head back up, his nose is spread across his face and blood pours down his chin.

"I'll ask you again, Sammy, where is your brother? And before you answer, think very carefully about how much you value the ability to eat and drink normally."

"Okay, okay, man. Fuck!" His chest heaves and fear lights his eyes. "Look, I don't know what he's done, man, but I haven't seen him in a couple of days."

Releasing my hold on his hair, I spin his stool to face me and snatch hold of his face in a crushing grip.

"You and I are going to have a serious fucking problem if you're lying to me," I say, downing the rest of my drink and slamming the glass on the bar. "If you see your waste of fucking space brother before me, tell him to start running. Because once I get hold of him, the only running he'll be able to do is in his fucking dreams. That clear?"

"Yeah, man. I got it," he croaks, holding his hands out to the side in submission.

I shove him away from me, and he almost topples off the stool but catches himself on the edge of the bar.

"Now get the fuck out of here." He gets to his feet, stumbling as he hurries away. "Fucking pussy," I mutter as Lila places another Old Fashioned in front of me and leaves a damp towel on the bar for me to clean the blood off my hand.

"You think he was telling the truth?" Zak asks, taking a seat.

"Fuck, no! I don't really give a shit. I'll catch up with him soon enough." I knock back my second drink of the night. I have a feeling it's going to be a long fucking one. "Keep'em coming, Lila."

And she does. I don't miss the longing looks she throws my brother's way every time she serves us another drink, or the way she scowls when Candi sidles up to Zak, scraping her claws down his exposed chest, and looking for a good time. I know he's been screwing Lila on and off for the past year, and I know it means more to her than it does him. There were even times when we shared her at the start. We've shared plenty of women, but none of them are *her*.

Roxanne Whitmore.

I wish I could say what comes next will be pleasant, will be a thrill, will be the making of us all. But it won't. What comes next has the power to not only destroy everything Roxy's worked for, but everything we did to get her there in the first place.

Chapter Three

Roxy

I watch as the second hand of the clock on the wall opposite my desk counts down the last few seconds to midnight. In another life, if I was another person, I might feel like Cinderella, but if only all I had to worry about was my carriage turning back into a pumpkin and my clothes turning back to rags at the stroke of midnight.

My worries aren't born of fairy tales, they are born of fucking nightmares. The work of minds more wickedly dark than the Brothers Grimm.

At exactly fifteen seconds past midnight, my phone pings with a message. I drop my eyes from the clock to my phone on the desk in front of me and read my final reminder.

Zak: Tick tock, Rox. Time to make your mind up.

Snatching my phone off the desk, I shove it in my bag and shut down my computer. Except for Smithy, who is knee deep in paperwork and calls out a weary goodnight to me as I pass, the office is empty.

Outside the station, I heave in a breath of cold night air, which catches in my lungs and makes me cough. Zak's message flashes in my mind as I stride across the car park.

Dropping into the car, I shove the key in the ignition and start the engine before pulling my phone out of my bag. I sit and stare at his message as the car warms and the windows begin to fog up before I type out a reply. My finger hovers over the send button, and I know once I send it there's no going back.

A moment later, the blare of a car horn makes me jump, taking my decision away from me as my phone chimes to indicate the message has been sent.

"Fucking hell!" I curse, dropping my head back against the headrest and banging it several times. With no other choice, I send another message.

Me: It's done!
Noah: You sure about this?
Me: Too late now. I'll message you later.

I delete the message thread before throwing my phone back in my bag and dumping it on the passenger seat, then I slam the car into gear and head towards Brick Lane.

As I drive, my mind drifts to the last time I saw Maddox and Zak up until two weeks ago. It was ten years ago, and the night my world fell apart in more ways than one.

That night plays out in my head as I turn off Brick Lane onto a small side street where Bishop's Bar is, and it's almost like I conjured them from my mind to appear in front of me. There they are casually leaning on the wall outside Bishop's waiting for me.

Ten years of pent-up emotion swarms me again; anger, grief, betrayal, and even a spark of the love I once felt for them stirs. All those emotions are obliterated by rage and hatred at the fact they are forcing me into a corner; forcing me to give up the one thing that means everything to me, my career.

Their eyes track me as I drive past, but I don't look their way once. I park my car at the side of the road several metres away from the bar.

Grabbing my bag, I dig around to find a mint to settle the nausea swirling up a storm in my stomach. Finally finding a packet, I shove the last two in my mouth and throw the wrapper back in my bag before snatching it up and climbing from the car.

The soles of my Dr Martens boots thud mutely around the empty street in time with the crunching of the mints in my mouth as I stride towards them.

Reaching them, I take them in. Maddox dressed in tight fitting black trousers and a leather jacket over a white shirt, open at the top, and I have to raise my head to look at his amber eyes, which narrow at my perusal of him. Zak is wearing a beautifully cut suit that does nothing to hide his well-toned but lean body. His blue eyes spark with something I can't quite read, and his messy blonde-brown hair is flopped to one side. Zak pushes off the wall and pulls the door to Bishop's open for me, and I arch a brow at him.

"Chivalry instead of bullets today. Now there's a turn-around, and more than a little out of character for you, don't you think," I say sarcastically and step through the open door. I feel Maddox as he steps in behind me and ignore the ripple of heat that flashes down my back.

"Have you forgotten everything we taught you, Roxanne," Maddox whispers to the back of my neck. I fight the shiver that's working its way free at his proximity and the heat of his breath on my skin.

"I haven't forgotten, Maddox. I know not to turn my back to my enemies. The problem with that is friend or foe, it doesn't matter, both are capable of inflicting fatal wounds. Maybe it's you who forgot." I step round the table, pulling out a chair and sit down. I don't miss the deep growl that comes from Maddox's direction, but I ignore it and him.

Zak pulls out the chair to the left of me, spinning it round before sitting on it, arms folded across the chair back. It's casual, relaxed. The sort of thing he used to do when we were kids, and it throws me for a second. Then I catch on to what he's doing. It's a psychological thing, to set me at ease, make me feel safe. If I were a lesser person, I'd fall for it, maybe even if I were the Roxy they knew before. But I'm not her.

Maddox on the other hand, sits in the chair directly opposite me. His intimidation tactics hard at play. Or so he thinks.

I finally take a look around the bar. It's one I know well, and exactly why I chose it. My eyes skim over the guy sitting in the back right corner, sipping his pint and pretending to read the paper. I keep my surprise at seeing him here locked up tight.

They have absolutely no idea who I am anymore or what I'm capable of.

I finally begin to relax, and when the waitress comes over, it's my turn to shock the shit out of them.

"Evening, Rox, the usual."

"Please, Demi, and can I get an Old Fashioned and Macallan on the rocks too."

"Of course. I'll bring them over."

I turn my attention back to the two men in front of me, and a beam of satisfaction lights at the scowl they are both wearing.

My small victory doesn't last long though.

"Get rid of the watchdog, Roxanne, or the deal is off," Maddox orders, and his scowl from moments earlier morphs into a triumphant smirk.

"I guess the deal is off then," I say, rising from my chair. A hand lands on my wrist, stopping me as chair legs scraping across the wooden floor signals others getting to their feet, including Maddox, who I snap my eyes to.

I hold my free hand up halting my watchdog, as Maddox called him, and give a shake of my head to ensure he understands.

Locked in a stare off with Maddox, I twist my hand in Zak's grip, and with a barely there nod from Maddox, Zak releases me.

Demi chooses that moment to arrive with our drinks and breaks the stalemate as Maddox and I take our seats again.

Drinks placed on the table, Demi hurries back to the bar, and I see Mitch ease back into his own chair. The fact he's been rumbled not bothering him in the slightest. It bothers the hell out me though.

"Looks like you forgot what's at stake, Roxanne," Maddox warns.

I shake my head, quirking a brow at him. "Not at all. I have a choice, even though you seem to be under the impression you have me by the balls."

He pitches forward, slamming his fist on the table in front of me. "There is no fucking choice. You do this or you risk losing everything," he snaps.

"Bullshit! I'm screwed no matter what I choose. But my choice remains. I just have to decide if it's me or you that ends my fucking career." I watch as my words hit home. He knows that either way, my time as a cop is done. After this goes down, I'll be cast from the force, stripped of everything I worked for, and be number fucking one on the most wanted list of every cop and criminal organisation across the damn country. "And I choose me, Maddox. Every fucking time because that's all I've got." I regret the vulnerability those words show, but they're the damn truth, and I'm all about the truth. It's the only reason I'm even agreeing to this. Allowing them to force my hand.

My need for truth and justice have been what fuelled me all those years ago. My need for answers to what happened to my mother and my sister have been the single thing to keep me from turning into the female version of the men before me.

It could so easily have been me sitting where they are, but I chose a different path ten years ago. One that led me to my best friend, Jessica, and helped me control the demon that resides inside me.

I know that doing this, stepping back into a world I left behind, will have her champing at the bit to be unleashed. I just hope I'm strong enough to prevent her from taking complete control and scorching the earth with her vengeance.

Chapter Four

Zak

It's almost three in the morning by the time my head meets my pillow, and it's thumping. Tonight was hard fucking work. Maddox is much better at hiding his truth.

My truth seeps out of me like the blood in my veins when you cut me. Rox might not have been around us for the last ten years, but I felt her eyes on me, searching out my little tells. Maddox is a fucking fool if he thinks she doesn't know shit about us. Her knowing our poison of choice proves that she's not as in the dark as we thought.

I enjoyed toying with her and sending her reminders of the ticking clock, but that was easy because I couldn't see her face, couldn't smell the scent of the perfume she's worn since we were teens wrapping around me. I was shocked as hell that she was still using it when we met her for the first time in the warehouse car park two weeks ago. The floral notes of lotus and lily and the woodsy scent of cedar and musk hit me almost as hard as leaving her behind did the night everything changed for us all.

I shake the thoughts from my head as the sound of the door opening downstairs reaches me. I know who it is, and

I'm in no mood for it. I slam my eyes shut at the first creak on the stairs and use the time it takes her to climb the stairs to settle my breathing into that of someone lost to sleep.

Maddox wasn't wrong when he called me a hypocrite earlier. In fact, he was bang on the fucking money, but at least my choice of pussy to get lost in isn't scraping the bottom of the barrel.

I'm all too aware that my days of fucking Lila are at an end. And if I'm honest, I've been waiting a long time for this day.

The click of my door opening echoes through the silent room, bringing a cool breeze from the hall with it. Goosebumps raise on my bared arms as muted footsteps travel over the plush carpet towards the bed.

When her fingertips meet my skin, I hold back the urge to flinch away from her. I know that I need to distance myself from her. I've been doing it subtly for months now.

"Zak?"

When I don't answer, I think she's got the message, but fuck no, she hasn't. The rustling of clothes being discarded perks my ears up, and when I feel the sheets lifting, I bolt up, bringing the knife I keep under my pillow with me.

"What the fuck do you think you're doing, Lila?" I ask, holding the blade beneath her chin, tip pointing upward. Her gasped squeal barely registers, and her wide eyes send a thrill of excitement through my whole body.

"Fuck, Zak. I thought—"

"Whatever you thought, unthink it. This is not what we do. Ever." I see her relax, but she's crazy if she thinks I won't hurt her. I push the tip up, just enough for her to know I'm fucking serious. My cock twitches at the whimper that expels from her, but I shove the lick of arousal away.

"Shit, okay. I'm going." She inches away from me, edging back out of the bed she stupidly thought she was invited into.

Shoving her clothes back on, she grumbles about what a crazy mother fucker I am, and I fight a smile.

As she turns toward the door, I call out, "Key, Lila. Give me the damn key."

She halts, turning back to me before digging into the pocket of her leather hot pants and pulling the key free. She strides towards me, and it feels as though she's the one brandishing the blade, stabbing through my flesh with every step.

"You're a fucking arsehole! I hope she's worth it," she fires at me, turning on her heels and walking away.

I bite back the retort sitting on the tip of my tongue, and only because I don't have time for clearing up blood and disposing of another body at this ridiculous time of night.

If it had been Maddox, she would have been dead before the words left her mouth. Not that murdering hapless females is his usual MO, but I think anything goes would have been more accurate after tonight.

I carefully place the blade back beneath the pillow as the front door slams shut downstairs. Light spills into the room through the now wide-open bedroom door, and I climb from the bed and close it just as a pleasurable scream rattles down the hallway.

Fucking Maddox.

I collapse back into my bed, throwing the other pillow over my head to drown out the onslaught of sex noises coming from two doors down. The walls in this place aren't thick enough for this shit.

I let my mind wonder back to tonight's meeting with Rox. I'm not surprised she chose to end her own career her way. She now has just under twenty-four hours to execute it, or shit is going to blow up for her big time. She wouldn't share details, but she assured us we'd know when it had happened.

Maddox isn't happy, but I warned him she would push back. And she has in typical Rox fashion. I'm quietly amused about the whole thing. Anything that pisses Maddox off tickles my warped sense of humour.

———

I'm in the small gym at our flat above Rogue, pounding the ever-loving shit out of the punch bag the next morning when Maddox bursts through the doors with murderous rage in his eyes and waving a newspaper in the air at me.

"Is she fucking crazy?" he rages, storming across to me.

I land another left jab before grabbing hold of the bag and resting my head on it. Blowing out a breath, I wait for him to elaborate. When he doesn't, I raise my head to look at him and narrowly miss being whacked as Maddox slams the newspaper on the punch bag where my head was just resting.

I scan the page before me, taking in the photo of what appears to be Rox accepting an envelope from a guy wearing a hoodie and whose face is hidden from view. The headline claims that she has resigned amid claims of corruption.

I shrug. "And?" I shove the paper off the bag and prepare to continue my workout.

"That's all you've got to fucking say."

Left, left, right. I pause my assault on the punch bag again.

"Yeah, it's all I've got to say. It's Rox, what did you expect? She knows what she's doing, Maddox. Besides, isn't this what we planned?" I shrug again and go back to hitting the bag before I hit my brother.

I watch as his eyes scan the paper again, huffing and puffing like the big bad wolf from *Little Red Riding Hood*.

"She did what you asked, man, just fucking leave it alone. It's not going to affect our plans, if anything it will help," I pant out between punches. He hears me, sighing deeply before turning and stomping back out the way he came.

After I finish in the gym, I take a quick shower and meet

happy with what you're doing. I know they have something on you, otherwise you'd never have thrown your career away like you have."

"Bye, Noah, and let me know when you find the stringer and identify who that guy with Rogers is." I walk away, shoving my sunglasses on as I exit the backstreet cafe.

Outside the sun is setting, and I quickly make it back to my car as the last rays of sun disappear behind a tower block.

I take a little detour on my way home and pass by the tattoo shop from Noah's list. I'm surprised to see a light on inside and pull over a little way up the road. I reposition my rear-view mirror so that the shop is in sight. I can see that it's actually two shops, but on one side the windows have been blacked out. There's nothing special about it, and it's fairly nondescript. Other than the name, there is nothing to give away what the shop is.

As I sit and watch the shop, I absent-mindedly run a hand over my left rib cage where my first tattoo sits and acts as a constant reminder to never trust anyone but myself again. Seventeen-year-old me really isn't so different to twenty-seven-year-old me. Sure, I'm older and supposedly wiser, and I'm certainly no longer so damn naive. But I'm still angry. I'm still hurting, although I don't show it or even admit it most of the time.

A hurt as deep as the one left by Maddox and Zak isn't easy to forget or to heal. Time just can't heal some wounds, and the scars those two boys left behind are jagged and raw. I know that every moment spent with them, near them, will rip them open again and again.

I switch the engine back on and shift the car into gear ready to pull away, but as I go to adjust my mirror back into position, a young girl, maybe early twenties, exits the shop. She's alone, and I watch as she locks up before heading off up the street.

On the way home, I can't keep my mind from running wild with questions about who she is. Is she just an employee? Or is she something more to one of them? Both of them?

I've heard the rumours over the years of how they like to share. Hell, at one point I could have been that girl. My teenage brain and rampant hormones had literally dreamt about it, wished for it, and I know it wasn't all one-sided. I'd seen the way they looked at me, felt the buzz beneath my skin whenever we touched, and I'd even shared a kiss, my first kiss, with Maddox *that* night.

Pulling up outside my house, I turn the engine off and drop my head back to the headrest with my eyes shut. A vision of Maddox and I laying on his bed swims behind them. The sweet smell of weed lingers in the air and on our clothes, and when he leans forward and his lips meet mine, I can taste alcohol and smoke. The combination is heady, and I remember the thrum between my legs as his tongue dipped inside, brushing against mine.

The moment was broken by a phone ringing, and it takes me a second to realise that my phone is actually ringing too. The vision blurs away as I focus my eyes on my lit-up phone sitting in its holder on the dash.

Snatching it up, I climb from the car and make my way inside, flicking lights on as I go. The hair on the back of my neck rises as I walk into the kitchen, and I know I'm not alone.

I don't bother with the light, it's not like I need it to see who it is. I already know. The tell-tale scent of cedar and smoke gave him away, and if it hadn't then the tense and dark atmosphere blanketing my kitchen would have.

"You think that little stunt you pulled with the press was a good idea? 'Cause I fucking don't. It's not what we discussed."

I drop my phone onto the counter and grab a glass.

This room is full of people that out on the street would kill one another in an instant. But not here.

Rocky nudges me, and I look to where his attention is focused. In a booth over on the left is Bonner, whose piercing gaze is already on me. There's a cruel smirk tilting the corner of his mouth.

Ignoring the glares and razor-sharp daggers coming at me, I stride across the room to Bonner.

"Maddox," he greets, gesturing to the seat across from him. I slide in as Rocky takes up position standing beside our table. Bonner eyes him, then looks to me. "No Zak this evening? What a disappointment." His words seem sincere, but the spark that lights in his eyes gives him away. He's happy it's just me, and suddenly I question whether Zak's absence was a play.

"He sends his apologies, but he had a better offer," I counter, watching as his eyes narrow at my words. "I have places to be, so how about you get to the fucking point."

He chuckles. "Patience, Maddox. It's a virtue you could do with having a lesson in." He picks up his bottle of beer from the table, taking a long drink before continuing, "This meeting is for your benefit more than mine. Maybe you'll even thank me."

"And maybe you'll drop dead right here, right now," I say with a derisive laugh.

"That's hardly polite—" I cut him off with a *don't fuck with me* look and a palm slammed to the table that draws attention from the next table. It also garners me some not so amused scowls from Bonner's two meathead muscle standing to the side. "Very well." He reaches into his jacket pocket, pulling a piece of paper free. Laying it down on the table, he slides it over to rest in front of me. "I believe this is one of your men?"

Slowly pulling my hardened gaze from Bonner, I look

down. Only it's not a piece of paper at all but a photo of Axel. My blood boils as what I'm seeing registers. Keeping my face neutral, I look up to Bonner with a nonchalant shrug.

"Your point?" I ask.

Bonner's brows raise at my blasé response. You don't need to be a genius to work out that Bonner was hoping for a little more from me.

"You don't seem surprised or even bothered by the fact one of your men is meeting with Rogers. And it looks like they're pretty cosy. If that was my man…" He trails off, leaving the rest of his sentence hanging.

I lean forward, resting my elbows on the table. "You got one of those photos in that pocket of yours of you kissing Rogers' arse too?" His eyes widen a fraction as his face pales a little before he covers it.

"How fucking dare you! I called you here in good faith, and you have the audacity to accuse me—"

My hand flies out, snatching hold of Bonner's shirt, curling it in my tightened fist and pulling him forward. There's a flurry of movement as Rocky and Bonner's meatheads step forward. Bonner raises a hand, halting them.

"Don't fucking bullshit me, Bonner. You told me I needed a lesson in patience, but you have no idea how patient I can be. You, however, are about to learn your own lesson in patience." I shove him away, rising from my seat and snatching up the photo from the table. As I go to walk away, one of Bonner's meatheads grabs my arm, pulling me back. I use the momentum, spinning on my heels, and slam my fist in his face. He stumbles back a few steps, cupping his nose as blood seeps through his fingers.

"Touch me again and I'll kill you." His friend laughs, and I can already see he thinks I'm joking. Turning to Bonner, I say, "Seriously?" He looks pleased with himself, and the reason

Slamming the bottle back on the counter, I stomp back to the lounge, snatching up my phone. I fire off a message to Noah letting him know I'm heading out for a while.

I know he's going to be pissed, but right now, I couldn't give one fuck.

Besides, there's no harm in a little reconnaissance. What trouble can I possibly get into just sitting in my car and watching?

I've been sat outside Rogue for the last hour with nothing of the least bit of interest. Obviously, if I was a guy then I'd be more than happy thanks to the fact that nearly every woman —some hardly that—is wearing a skirt barely covering their arse. Oh, how I wish I could bleach my eyes after one bent down to adjust her shoe, giving me a completely unrestricted view of her vajayjay. Needless to say, there were a number of toots from cars passing by.

I check the time on my phone, ignoring the message I know is from Noah, to see it's almost midnight. I've seen no sign of Maddox or Zak. Needing some fresh air, I open the glove box and take out the pack of fags I keep in there. Climbing from the car, I lean up against it and take a cigarette out as I watch a couple come stumbling out of Rogue. I place the cigarette between my lips as they disappear round the side of the building, not completely out of sight, and begin to make out.

I look away, enjoying the taste and scent of tobacco on my tongue. I don't smoke anymore, but I like to reminisce occasionally.

Movement across the road catches my eye, and I look over to see another guy has joined the couple round the corner. They pull her away from the wall before sandwiching her in between them both, hands roaming all over each other, and a small wanton moan carries on the night air.

Not going to lie, it's hot. My libido is awake and fully alert. I'm so engrossed in the trio, that I don't notice the guy approaching me from the left.

"You open for business," he slurs, almost losing his balance as he falls against the car next to me. Startled, the fag falls from my mouth to the ground. He reaches out a hand to my arm, and I knock it away.

"How about you go home, hey," I tell him, dodging his wondering hands and trying to direct him off down the road without drawing attention.

"How 'bout...you come with me, huh? A hot little th-thing like you's probably got a sweet cunt," he groans, grabbing at his crotch and thrusting his hips. The movement causes him to totter clumsily further into the road. I roll my eyes at the drunken moron.

"Seriously? You can barely stand, let alone get it up," I mumble, stepping forward to stop him from falling over completely. The screeching of tyres has my head snapping to the right as a car skids round the corner before heading straight for him. The headlights make it difficult to see, and I blindly throw out a hand trying to catch hold of him. My fingers brush something, but before I can get a grip on it, it falls away. Then everything happens in slow motion.

The car slows a second before gunfire lights up the street, and I watch as bullets meet flesh. A bouncer outside Rogue, a young girl in the line and the trio at the side of the building. All of them rear back from the impact before falling to the ground. There's a thud as the car passes me by, and I catch a glimpse of the back of two men, the driver and his back seat passenger, each with their arm out the window and firing guns.

As the car screeches off down the road, I grab my phone

from inside the car and call it in. With my phone to my ear, I step forward only to stop when I see a figure sprawled out in the road. Walking towards it, I watch for any movement or signs of life but there are none. I place the call on speaker, telling the operator what I need as I turn my phone torch on and direct the beam of light to the man.

Crouching at his side, the light from my phone glints off a pool of blood beneath the man's head. I place two fingers on his neck, seeking the pulse that should be there. Not finding one, I let out a sigh and rise before jogging across the road.

As people pour out of the building and see the carnage and bodies littering the floor, several screams rent through the air. I look to the bouncer who is slumped on the ground holding his hand to a wound in his shoulder. Seeing he's still breathing, my eyes trail to the young girl from the queue. She's not moving, and as I move towards her the reason becomes obvious. Her eyes are lifeless and staring up to the night sky, and there between them is a bullet hole. I step back, preparing to check the trio from the side of the building when I'm jostled from behind as more people emerge from inside now that the threat seems to have passed.

Sirens blare in the distance, and I begin to move everyone to the other side of the road before making way back to check the other victims. Just as I reach the side of the building, a hand latches onto my arm and yanks me back.

Spinning around ready to smack the fucker, I meet dark stormy eyes that tell of a thousand deaths. He pulls me to the entrance and inside, then through another door and into an office, slamming the door behind him. He releases me instantly like I burned him and stomps away from me.

"What the fuck are you doing here, Roxanne?"

Chapter Eight

Zak

I pull up outside Axel's and shoot him a text to let him know I'm here. I watch several teens in the estate park larking about. Two of the lads are wrestling while another is busy tagging the slide in a vivid shade of green spray paint. Two girls are sat huddled inside a makeshift hut attached to the slide, their heads close together as they chat and smoke.

The faces of the teens blur into the faces of us; Maddox, me and Rox. We grew up on an estate like this doing just what they are doing now. Shooting the shit and causing trouble. I'd like to think that the kind of trouble these guys get into is a lot less dangerous than ours, although I doubt not.

Maddox and I were bad boys. We still are. When your childhood consists of beatings from whichever prick your mother is screwing and almost dying when you took something you thought were sweets but turned out to be ecstasy, then yeah, being a bad boy seems like an obvious evolution. Being quite literally dragged away from the only parent you've ever known, albeit a bad one, is bound to leave you emotionally traumatised.

Those sorts of things leave an indelible mark on your skin, on your mind and on your soul.

I look away from the teenagers as the main door to Axel's block opens, and he steps out. Spotting me, he jogs over and jumps in the car.

"Hey, man. Sorry 'bout that, I fell asleep. So, where we off to?"

"Rogue," I reply and give nothing more than that as I turn the car around. I don't miss the furtive glances he keeps throwing towards his building. He seems skittish, so when I look back through the rear-view mirror and spot a young, dark-haired woman exiting the block, a woman who stands out like a sore fucking thumb dressed as she is, my suspicions raise.

Sometimes fate throws you a helping hand, and I stop the car for an old lady to cross the road. During the time it takes for her to amble across, I watch as the dark-haired woman climbs into a black Fiesta. It's a newer model and certainly not something most who live here can afford.

When she pulls up behind me, I swear Axel's body goes rigid.

"What has you so tired? You have a late one last night?" I probe casually.

"Nah, the fucking couple next door kept me up half the night arguing. You know those walls are like fucking paper. When they finally finished, the screwing started. Crazy bitch could give a porn star a run for her money the noise she was making." Not content with his description, he demonstrates. "'*Ahhh, fuck me harder, Billy. Yes! Yes!*'" he yells in a mock high-pitched female voice.

I can't help laughing at him as he continues, even adding breathy pants. I try to get a better look at the chick behind us, but it's dark out making it impossible to see clearly. Getting her number plate is the best I can do.

I've been up in the office watching the CCTV for the last few hours and keeping a careful watch on Axel too. I tasked him with mingling, blending into the crowd and watching for any of Laskin's men. Not that I think he's stupid enough to send his dealers inside Rogue, but Laskin's getting more and more brazen.

I'm sorting through paperwork when my attention is caught by something on the camera outside. The office is sound proofed, but I don't need sound to know what's going on.

My chair falls to the floor as I jump up, racing for the door. Screams and the sound of gunfire slam into me the instant the door opens.

Entering the main room, people are running in all directions or hiding beneath tables as gunfire continues to rain outside and inside as glass from the windows explodes, showering people and the floor. Several people hit the ground while others trip and fall in their rush to flee. I spot Axel herding people to safety behind the bar and flipping tables to create a shield as I duck and dash across the floor.

The gunfire ceases as the door leading to the storeroom and back exit opens, revealing Maddox with Rocky trailing behind him.

I watch as Maddox's eyes scan the room, hardening as he spots the bodies on the floor. His nostrils flare, and I can feel his rage like a tangible thing. When they land on me, I see the relief on his face. It's only there for a second before his face hardens again, and he stomps this way.

As he reaches me, a woman steps out from a table she'd been hiding behind, gripping onto her friend's hand, and lets out a piercing scream when her eyes land on a body lying feet from her in pool of blood.

Before either of us can stop her, she races for the door, dragging her friend by the hand behind her, hysterically and causing panic. Others emerge from their hiding places and begin frantically trying to exit.

"Fucking hell!" Maddox exclaims, running a hand over his stubble covered jaw. "Zak, get the rest of these people out of here," he orders before striding for the front exit.

I do as he says, leading terrified woman and even some guys, who look like they might piss themselves any second, to the exit. Rocky checks over those with injuries, moving the ones still breathing to a corner of the room. I hear sirens and look up just as I see Maddox dragging someone through to the office.

Once everyone is out, except those who are hurt, I quickly head to the office after Maddox. I didn't get a good look at the woman, but I didn't need to. I would recognise her anywhere.

Not able to hear anything from the soundproofed room, I quietly open the door to find Maddox facing off against Rox, who has her back to me and is spitting fire at him.

"Excuse me? Your club just got shot the fuck up and you're worried about what I'm doing here. Pfft." She waves a dismissive hand at him before starting back in at him. "I think you should be more concerned about the police that are going to be crawling all over this place any minute. Not worrying about the cop—sorry ex-cop, standing in front of you who is wondering what the actual fuck she's been dragged into, *Maddox*," she spits, stepping forward and jabbing a finger into his chest.

Maddox's eyes light with a mixture of fury and respect at the woman standing there with not an ounce of fear evident in her at all.

She'd always been fearless. The day we met her she was getting her arse beat on by some little prick called Wayne from the estate. We had watched her land a couple of decent punches to his face before he laid into her. I guess we saw something of ourselves in her, something that spoke to us on a base level, and that's why we helped her.

Maddox's hand swipes out, snatching her wrist and easily encasing it within his large hand. He yanks her forward, causing her body to crash into his.

"Remember who you're talking to, Roxanne. We aren't the same people anymore, and you'd do well to remember that." She lifts her chin at his words, and I can picture the defiance in her eyes at his threat. He forces her back several steps, and I straighten from my position leaning against the door frame as her back comes to within an inch of me.

Her breath catches and her shoulders broaden as she feels me behind her. I look at Maddox over her head, seeing the devilish glint in his eyes.

"Hey, Rox," I whisper in her ear, before running my tongue over the shell and taking a little nip too, just for good measure. Her head moves a fraction, but it's just enough to tell me how much being sandwiched between the two of us has affected her.

"Fuck you. Fuck you both!" she snarls in response, but there's little heat in it. Not the kind she intended anyway.

Maddox grins and lets out a deep rumble of laughter, only infuriating her more. The laughter dies, his face becoming a mask as he says, "You'll get your chance. It's on the agenda." He releases her quickly, and she stumbles back.

My hands automatically go to her hips to steady her, and she growls out her frustration at being manhandled and at Maddox's insinuation that she'd fuck us both.

Maddox walks past us to the door, turning at the last second. "Stay put, Roxanne," he orders, before calling me to follow with a nod of his head.

I watch as her breathing changes, almost panting, and the pulse in her neck speeds up at Maddox's order.

"How turned on are you right now, Rox?"

"Not at all," she scoffs, like it's the most ridiculous thing she's ever heard. "Get your fucking hands off me before you no longer have the use of them."

"Liar," I say, calling her out as I give a little tug on her hips, bringing her body flush with mine. "If I were to slip a hand beneath those tight as fuck trousers of yours, I know you'd be as wet as I am hard, Rox." I run my hand over her abdomen to her waistband, making her think that's exactly what I intend to do, but at the last minute, I pull back, letting her go. I don't even wait for her to catch her breath before I follow Maddox, closing the door behind me.

I'm hard as fucking granite and know she felt every damn inch of it brush up against her perfectly rounded arse. Damn! I quickly adjust myself before stepping out into the main room. Just as well I did too. The room is overrun with cops and paramedics, even the coroner is here.

I spot Maddox talking to a cop over on the left side of the room, and I quickly look around for Rocky or Axel. Not finding either of them, I make my way over to Maddox, knowing that I'll need to give a statement and wanting it done as quickly as possible.

It's several hours before the place is cleared out and ready to be locked up. The cops have left, and the final board is being fitted over the last broken window when I find myself standing outside the office.

Maddox joins me and asks what I was already wondering. "You think she's still here?"

"Only one way to find out," I say, grasping the door handle and pushing inside.

The room is empty, as we both suspected it would be.

There is no way Rox would have stayed, especially seeing as it was Maddox that told her too. Even as a teen, she had a problem with authority. Fuck knows how she ever became a cop.

Growing up the way she did—we did—it's not a surprise. When you have to look after yourself if you want to eat and stay alive, you grow up fast. Add to that having to raise your own sister and what you end up with is a head-strong and independent woman with a streak so fierce that you'd have to be mentally unstable to even think about crossing her.

I guess that places Maddox and I squarely in the mentally unstable category after what we did to her. But there was a very good reason, and one she'll uncover soon enough.

Chapter Nine

Roxy

I spin around as the door closes behind me, letting out a growl of frustration and cursing my stupid fucking body for its reaction. I look around the room, taking in the desk, filing cabinets and monitors showing the main floor, the corridor to the toilets and outside, which is a hive of activity as police and paramedics hurry about doing their jobs.

I ignore the pang in my chest at the fact I'm not there along with my colleagues investigating a drive-by and am instead standing in an office and watching as a civilian who came close to becoming just another dead body in another pointless street vendetta.

Unfortunately, the thought has already manifested in my brain, making my anger at this situation rise to boiling point. Don't even get me started on the shit Maddox spouted from his mouth. A mouth that could set a thousand fires alight, both verbally and physically. I'd be insane to try and ignore that the years have been more than kind, and the teen boy I once knew has grown in *every* way. And it's clear he's not the only one. Zak has grown too. Only his growth comes with more depth, and now, he's like some sort of Japanese puzzle box, a very fucking complex one.

I shake off the tingling still coursing through my body from their close proximity and begin to move around the room. The filing cabinets aren't locked, and that tells me there's nothing important in them, which is confirmed when I have a quick skim through. Nothing but employee records and invoices. Moving to the desk, it's clear except for an open laptop and a ledger with monthly figures. They're nothing to be sniffed at either. Maddox and Zak are making a tidy little package here.

I take a seat, leaning back as a stretcher with a body covered by a white sheet is wheeled out and loaded into a van. No matter how many times I see it, it's an image that throws me back ten years.

"Just go, guys, I'll be fine. I'll catch up with you tomorrow," I say, trying to sound casual but missing the mark by a mile. I'm fiddling with the zip of my worn jacket and rocking on my toes as I stand before Maddox and Zak.

Zak steps forward, pulling me into a hug, either unaware or glossing over the awkward tension filling the air between Maddox and me.

"See you tomorrow, Rox. Take care of you," he whispers, squeezing me tighter and holding on a little longer than necessary. Stepping back, he makes room for Maddox, who shuffles forward, taking his place.

We go to embrace, our arms crashing into one another's, then switching positions at the same time and doing it again. We both snigger, and the tension is released.

"See you later, Roxanne." His voice rumbles across the shell of my ear, worming its way deep into my body. And my heart. As he begins to pull away, I feel his lips brush the side of my face,

and I don't even try to hide the shiver that runs over my whole body as the light caress becomes a firm kiss planted at the corner of my mouth.

When he releases me, I watch as something sullen passes in his eyes, like this is a final goodbye, but it's gone before I can think on it too much, and a small smile lines his lips. I turn away from them, jogging up the path and into my block.

I skip the lift and head for the stairwell, needing the extra time to process everything that happened tonight. My fingers involuntarily trace my bottom lip, and I almost miss the top step lost in my memories. I still can't believe Maddox kissed me. Among all those dizzy first kiss feelings are a riotous number of mixed emotions too. It would be so easy if I didn't have feelings for Zak too, but I do.

How can I have feelings for two boys at once? Not just any two boys either, but brothers, who also happen to be my best friends.

My thoughts are thrown aside as the warm, fuzzy feelings from moments ago are replaced by a sick, unnerving stirring in the pit of my stomach that has the hairs on my neck rising.

Finally looking up and taking in my surroundings, I see my flat up ahead, but the door is ajar, and unease swirls like a whirlwind, flipping my gut on its head.

As I draw level with my door, I can see the dim light from the lounge filtering through the gap along with the sound of the TV.

A gust of wind whistles down the communal walkway, throwing up dried leaves and blowing them along the ground.

"Mum?" I call out, reaching out a hand to the door. Just as my fingertips make contact, a loud bang echoes up the stairwell behind me making me jump and clutch my chest as I spin around. The sound of laughter trickles up from below before drifting away as a door closes, locking the sound inside.

"Fuck!" I blow out a breath, a thimbleful of relief washing

over me. Turning back to my flat, I call out again, "Mum? Star?" Pushing inside, an unpleasant, metallic scent tickles my nose, causing me to scrunch it up in disgust.

I pass the kitchen, noticing the half-peeled veg left on the counter. As my eyes trail over everything, I notice several red splotches on the floor and follow them as they continue past me and into the lounge.

I rub my hands up and down my arms, trying to fight the feeling of dread that is now wild and free in my body. There's no door on the lounge, so images from the TV flicker across the floor. Taking a step forward, I can now see the arm of the sofa and resting, as though the person it belongs to is sleeping, is one slippered foot. As I look closer, my skin prickling, I notice the slipper is at an odd, almost, right angle, and there are red smears across the heel of the foot.

"Mum," I call out, my voice cracking with worry. Another step closer has the other foot coming into view, resting on the floor.

Shaking off the fear licking my body, I rush into the lounge falsely believing that because Mum is here everything is okay.

My forward motion grinds to halt as the full scene is revealed to me, and I skid on something warm and wet, landing on my arse. My hands make a splat sound as they hit the carpet, and the air rushes from my lungs in a harsh breath.

A scream catches in my throat, blocking my air way, and I scramble backwards on my arse and hands, unable to gain any traction with my feet.

My back hits something hard, and I realise I'm against the sideboard that the TV is mounted on. My breath comes in pants as my brain tries to catch up with what my eyes are looking at. It's like stepping into the house cast me into an 80s slasher movie, and everywhere I look is more horrific than the last.

My mind knows there's no hope she's alive, but it doesn't stop me from crawling to her on my hands and knees. When I reach *her, I raise up on my knees and reach out a hand to her face, eyes half open and swollen, lip split and blood...so much blood. A sob rips from my throat, turning to a wretched scream that could shatter the window of every flat in the block.*

"Mum," I whisper, turning her face towards me. "Oh my god, Mum," I cry, tears falling unabated. I'm hesitant, unsure where to touch her as everywhere seems to have an injury. Barely able to see through the tears, I feel her neck, checking for the little thrumming beat that indicates life. Not finding one, I try to convince myself I must be doing it wrong instead of admitting what I know deep down in my heart. After five more minutes and still no pulse, I drop back on my hunches.

As reality washes over me, I'm faintly aware of sirens in the background, but I pay no mind, instead remaining where I am and staring at my hands, which I now see are painted in blood. I don't know how long I sit there before the face of my sister swims in my mind.

I scramble to my feet, head whipping back and forth round the room, seeking her out. Not finding her anywhere, and there being nowhere for her to hide in here, I walk determinedly back to the hall and climb the stairs, calling out to her and leaving a trail of bloody foot and hand prints in my wake.

"Star. Star, where are you?" I frantically search each room, tearing clothes from wardrobes and checking every possible hiding place for an eight-year-old girl. Finding nothing, I hurry back downstairs to check the kitchen and the cupboard under the stairs.

As I step out of the empty cupboard, I come face to face with a police officer, arm raised holding his baton ready to strike.

"Police. Don't move," he shouts to me, holding his other hand out, palm up in warning.

"You need to find her. Please find her. She's only a baby. Where is she?" It's at this point that my ability to make sense, to

function, to even stand begins to crumble, and rationality and fear have well and truly left as I collapse to the floor.

The police officer is talking to me, and I'm aware of movement around me, but I can't hear him and don't look up, even when hands wrap around me, lifting me up and carry me from the building.

I'm sitting in the back of an ambulance, doors wide open, as a paramedic checks me over. It could be five minutes or five hours when two men wheeling a stretcher pass by. As they roll over the uneven ground, the stretcher jolts, and a hand flops down, falling free from the white sheet covering them.

My phone ringing snaps me out of the memory, and I pull it free to see Mitch's name flashing across the screen.

Anxiety ripples like a wave through my gut as I answer the call. "Mitch." I don't bother with pleasantries.

"It's not her, Roxy."

"Fuck!" The word rushes out of me before he's finished talking, and I breathe a deep sigh of relief. It's a bittersweet relief though because if it's not her, it's someone's daughter, and equally, it means that she's still out there.

"Roxy, you okay? Where are you?" Mitch's voice holds a note of worry, and I'm quick to dispel his concern.

"I'm good. Just out grabbing some food."

"At this time of night?" he queries, and as I look to my watch, I understand why. It's almost one in the morning.

"I couldn't sleep, so I thought I'd grab a late-night snack, but I'm going home now." The lie falls easily from my lips, but it sits like concrete in my stomach. I hate lying to Mitch, and over the last ten years, I can count on one hand the number of lies I've told him and his wife, Simone.

Mitch was the cop that found me that night. He'd only been on the job a couple of years, and it was his first homicide.

One he'll never forget. He checked up on me several times after that night, and even drove me to my new foster home. I didn't last there long. In fact, I didn't last anywhere long after that, unless you count the back of a police car or holding cell at the station. If people thought I was a troubled teen before that night, they hadn't seen anything. I was wild and unrepentant in my grief.

"Hey, you still there?" Mitch calls down the line.

"Shit. Sorry, yeah, I'm still here, but I've got to go, food is ready. I'll call you tomorrow."

"Okay, Roxy. Take care."

"I will, you too. Thanks, Mitch," I say sincerely. There's no snark, no attitude, just truthful love and respect for the man that saved me.

Ending the call, I stand and shove my phone back in my pocket before walking to the door. Screw this shit. I'm not sitting here like some fucking loyal dog. My current situation might all be down to Maddox and Zak, but I still don't take fucking orders and will do this my way. Besides, they haven't earned anything from me except a nice double plot in the cemetery.

Chapter Ten

Zak

I wake around midday with a banging headache, and I'm not entirely sure how much of that is lack of sleep or down to the vast amount of alcohol I consumed last night. Well, early hours of this morning to be more precise.

After clearing up from the shooting, then discovering that Rox had done her infamous disappearing act, I needed a drink or ten. They went down like a damn dream while Maddox filled me in on his meet up with Bonner. I know he kept something back from me, and normally I wouldn't be concerned. He's my brother and though we don't usually keep secrets, there have been times over the years where he's omitted telling me certain things. Right now, his silence is a worry.

The flat is silent as I head for the shower. I wasn't in any state to make it back to our house last night, so I crashed at the flat above Rogue again. Stepping into the kitchen, feeling slightly less hungover, I find a note on the fridge from Maddox letting me know there's a delivery due this morning. Grabbing a quick breakfast, consisting of burnt toast and a cup of black tea because there's no milk, I then head downstairs.

The club is darker than usual thanks to the boarded-up

windows, and I flip a few lights on as I walk around. There's a bang at the front door as I dump our glasses from last night in the sink. I begin walking slowly to the door, assuming it's the delivery, and in no hurry when another bang booms through the empty space. Only this time they don't stop, and the banging continues becoming increasingly more demanding along with a muffled shout from the other side.

"Hold the fuck on!" I yell as I reach the door, sliding the top and bottom bolts across and pulling the handle. I don't need to pull very hard. The door practically flies open as a body comes tumbling in with it.

"What the fu—" My words cut off as a groan drifts up from the heap on the floor at my feet, and as they roll onto their back, I see it's Axel. "Shit, man. What the fuck happened to you?" I say, hooking my arms beneath his and pulling him in the rest of the way so I can close the door. He groans and winces the whole time. Slamming the door shut and locking it, I turn back to Axel, still prone on the floor where I left him. I finally get a proper look at him, and he looks like he went ten rounds with Fury without the gloves. His eye is swelling shut, he has a split and fat lip and a large gash on his temple. His clothes, which are the same ones he had on last night, are dirty and torn, and I imagine the rest of his body looks like his face.

I pull my phone from my pocket and shoot Maddox a message telling him we have a situation and to get back here as soon as.

"Where's Maddox?" he asks, his voice hoarse. He lays a hand over his left side, grimacing as he tries to sit up, and I step behind him to help.

"He's out. What the hell happened, Axel?"

"I need to speak to him now." This time his voice is a little stronger with a demanding undertone.

"Answer the damn question, Axel?" I demand back.

He sighs, swiping a hand over his mouth and wincing as

he brushes his split lip. Just when I think he isn't going to answer me, he speaks.

"What did he tell you about his meeting with Bonner?"

I frown, remembering my thoughts earlier about Mad keeping things from me. "Enough," I reply, deliberately being vague.

He nods. "So, you know about me meeting Rogers." His face falls, and I hear him muttering and taking several deep breaths before looking back up at me. I keep my mask in place, not giving anything away. "He knows, Zak. He knows what you're doing, and he isn't going to go without a fight."

Anger sparks in the small part of my brain that deals with emotions, the Amygdala. I may not have finished school or attended often, but I read a lot. I needed something for my brain to focus on, an escape from my memories, the worst ones at least, and reading was it. Most of the guys we know can barely spell their own name let alone read a damn book. I know the process and how the brain reacts to anger, but I also know how to control it, manipulate it to my advantage.

"And how the fuck would he know that, Axel." I keep my tone measured and calm, hiding any hint of the real emotions flooding my system right now. When he speaks next, his words aren't a surprise.

He looks straight at me, almost taunting me. "Because I told him, Zak. Me. I fucking told him everything." There's defiance in his eyes, but I see the pain of his betrayal and what he's done too. It's a shame that neither of those things will keep him alive.

Before he can say another word, my fist connects with his face.

I'm just closing the door behind the delivery man when my phone rings. Pulling it free from my pocket, I quickly answer it.

"What you got, man?" Guessing I'm in no mood for niceties, he gets on with it.

"Her name is Eva Trent, 25, lives in Camden. I'll send you the address. Otherwise, her record is clean."

"Cheers," I say, ending the call. I make a note to find time to pay her a visit and find out who she is to Axel, especially in light of his earlier confession. Something makes me think she's of some importance.

I spend the rest of the day sorting out the replacement of the new windows and throwing a couple of backhanders to the relevant people to ensure Rogue can open tonight.

At around five, the bar manager, Chase, arrives along with a couple of the bar staff. After a quick chat about what happened last night, I disappear off to meet Maddox.

When I arrive at the docks, I find Maddox chatting to Bowser. They finish up just as I stop next to Maddox, and Bowser gives me a nod in greeting before heading back off to the warehouse.

"Where is he?"

"I had Rocky take him to the house and secure him downstairs." Maddox begins walking towards the car, and I follow behind him. "Why didn't you tell me?"

"I have my reasons. Now let's go."

After I knocked Axel out, I called Maddox. He didn't give me details over the phone because that would be fucking stupid, but he told me to have the package delivered to the house.

"Bad day at the office?" I jest as we reach the car and both climb in. Maddox doesn't answer, just side-eyes me with a grunt. Deciding not to push him, I ask, "And last night, what's the word on that?"

Wheel spinning onto the main road, narrowly missing a car, Maddox slams the car into third and tears off down the street.

"Not a fucking peep. And with no sign of Laskin's crew last night, that tells me he knew something was going down at the very fucking least."

"This is not his style. The guy has assassins for hire. There's no fucking way he'd shoot up Rogue." We drive in silence for the next thirty minutes. As we pull up to the gates to our home, I ask, "What about the tip off from Ripley, where did that come from?"

"I checked with him this morning," he says, stopping in the garage. "He has a mate in the Acers. They go way back, and Ripley trusts him, despite who he runs with."

The Acers are a pain in our fucking arse, but they aren't a big threat to us. A small outfit that have gained a bit of traction in the last year thanks to Rogers taking out their main rivals. No doubt the guy has an ulterior motive, he always fucking does, but so far, the Acers have managed to remain outside of the main trifecta that pulls the strings of London like a damn puppet.

Inside the house, we find Rocky in the kitchen talking to Maria, the housekeeper, and stuffing his face. The house is full of the aroma of roasted lamb, rosemary and garlic, and there's the sweet and unmistakable scent of melted chocolate.

"Ah, here are my boys. Just in time for a nice roast," Maria states, stepping round the island to give each of us a hug.

"Hey, Maria. Something smells delicious." I release her, and she goes to check the pans on the hob.

I watch from the corner of my eye as Rocky gives Maddox a nod, letting him know that everything is ready.

"Get washed up, boys. Dinner will be ready in ten minutes." Mad goes to speak, but she stops him. "Dinner first, then business. He's been there all day, a little while longer won't hurt. Now, come."

I stifle a laugh, giving Rocky a slap on the back as I pass.

Maria and her husband, Arthur, used to work for Rogers' father Theo, and had been with the family for years. After Theo was murdered and Rogers took over, he got rid of a lot of Theo's most loyal men.

About six months after Theo's death, Arthur went missing. He was gone for several more months before his body turned up floating down the Thames. When we heard what had happened, we moved Maria in here with us. The woman had lost everything. For as long as I can remember, she was a part of our lives. Cooking and cleaning, and even fixing us up too if we got hurt whilst on a job. I've no doubt this woman could put a lot of men, us included, behind bars for a very long time with the information she knows and the things she's seen over the years.

Despite Maddox's impatience to get to business, he does as she asks, and we eat dinner first.

Chapter Eleven

Roxy

I gently remove the arm that's laying across my body, trying not to wake him, and slip from the bed. Closing the bathroom door behind me, I lean against it and stare at the ceiling for several seconds, silently berating myself for being so stupid last night.

I climb into the shower and turn it on, wincing as the icy-cold water rains down on me. When I arrived home last night, Noah was here waiting for me in his car. To say he was pissed at me would be a slight understatement. But it's nothing to how I was feeling. Unfortunately, amongst all the other emotions that were warring in my body, horny was top of the list. I had planned to come home and quite literally send myself into an orgasm induced coma. So, when we got inside and Noah was spouting about how irresponsible I was and how I could have got hurt or ruined everything, I couldn't help myself as he stepped into me, wrapping me in his arms.

The water warms, and as it snakes down my tired body, I'm reminded of Noah's lips, tongue and teeth as they trailed and explored me last night. Only, just like last night, it's not him I picture when I close my eyes.

No, my imagination has fallen head over heels with the idea Maddox salaciously whispered in my ear last night.

Traitor. Traitorous body and mind.

I quickly wash, barely skimming my body so as not to ignite anymore lust driven thoughts about Maddox and Zak.

I'm just rinsing off the last of the conditioner from my hair when I hear the bathroom door opening and see Noah slipping inside. I promptly switch the shower off and climb out, snatching the towel hanging to the side and wrap it around me while Noah is busy taking a leak. I'm not sure when we went from hooking up to suddenly using the loo in front of one another, but I don't fucking like it.

Finished relieving himself, he turns to me. "Morning." His voice has a sleepy morning husk to it, and his hands reach out to draw me to him, but I brush them aside, stepping away from him.

"What are you doing, Noah? This is not us." I grab another towel and begin drying my hair as I move to leave the room.

"Come on, Rox, we're good together. Last night surely proved that to you," he says, following me back into the bedroom.

I throw the towel I was using to dry my hair on the unmade bed and move to the dresser, taking out a pair of knickers and a bra.

"No, Noah, all last night showed me is that this can't happen again." I slip the knickers on, then drop the towel and put my bra on. "I need to be somewhere, so..." No need for me to finish as my meaning is clear.

"Hey," he says, grabbing my arm and spinning me to face him. "What the fuck, Rox? You're throwing me out?"

I look down at the hand wrapped around my bicep, then back to him as I yank away from his hold. "No, Noah, not literally, but fucking lay your hands on me again, and it can be arranged. I told you the other day, what's between us is work and the occasional fun in the bedroom. Clearly, that's not the case for you anymore, so this"—I wave a hand between us—"won't be happening again. And I'll say it again, just in case you didn't get it the last time, if you can't do your job without letting the fact we had sex get in the way then you need to walk away now."

He starts collecting his clothes and pulling them on before he even looks at me again.

"You already know my decision, but that doesn't mean I have to be happy about it. I'll be in touch about the shooting when I know more. See you later, Rox." He storms from the house, slamming the door behind him.

I finish getting dressed before stripping the bed and putting clean sheets on. Chucking it all in the washing machine and wishing it was as easy as that to wash away my stupidity for going there again with Noah when I knew he was starting to want more from me.

After a quick bite to eat and a much-needed coffee, I spend the rest of the morning going over everything that Noah gave me the other day again.

Noah told me last night that they still don't have an ID of the guy in the pictures or the stringer. Still finding nothing of much use and needing some air, I decide to go and do the food shop I should have done two days ago.

A few people openly stare at me in the supermarket but most just avoid me. The lady at the checkout visibly turns her nose up at me as the previous customer moves away and I reach the till.

"Afternoon," she greets, and whilst there's a smile on her face, her tone does little to cover her dislike of me.

"Hey," I greet back with a smile on my face. Kill the haters with kindness, right? I load my shopping and pay without another word said between us.

As I pick my bags up, the cashier leans forward and snarls, "You should be ashamed of yourself. Dirty pig."

I pause, turning back to her and running my gaze over her. It makes her uncomfortable, which pleases me. I check her name badge, Lydia, and look her over again. After a moment I remember why she seemed familiar.

"How's your brother, Lydia? I hear The Scrubs is better these days, safer," I retort with a wink, only I don't whisper like she did, and the small group around us, including several of her colleagues, gasp and begin whispering. "You know, glass houses and all that jazz. Bye, Lydia."

I walk out of the supermarket with my head held high. They don't know the truth, and most of them couldn't give two shits. Even before my fabricated corruption story broke, cops weren't respected as they should be.

Lydia's brother, Thomas, is now serving life for murder. The lad was only eighteen and will now spend the best years of his life behind bars all for the glory and prestige he and others like him believe being part of a gang brings. I'm not judging because nowadays it's kill or be killed. It's a shocking ethos to live life by, but it's a real one when you grow up on the poorest estates.

On my way home, I find myself taking a detour and pulling up at my old estate. I haven't been back here in years, but it hasn't changed much at all.

It reminds me of the film *Harry Brown*, and just like in the movie, the entrance to the underpass opposite the flats is occupied by a group of youths harassing every passer-by and selling to those that want something for letting loose on a Saturday night.

Tears well in my eyes as I'm assaulted by memories. Some are good but most are painful, and when a young girl, around nine or ten, walks passed, there's no stopping the tears that fall. She reminds me of Star.

My baby sister, Anastasia, was the most important thing in my life, and the one person I would have done anything for and frequently did too. I called her Star because that was what she was to me, the bright light in a dark world.

The night my mother was murdered, Star had been at the house with her. I know this because I'd spoken to her after school and made sure she'd gotten home okay. But when I got there and found my mother's body, there was no sign of her.

There have been a few possible leads over the years but nothing solid, and even though they found traces of her blood at the scene that night, I refuse to give up looking for her. I refuse to leave her out there, dead or alive.

Spinning the car around, I head home. My mind is full of questions, questions I've asked myself a hundred times or more over the years. None of the answers my mind conjures are good.

As I turn down my road, I come to a stop, unable to go any further. The whole road is blocked, and the paths are lined with residents. Smoke plumes in the sky, spiralling upwards and carried away by the wind that's picked up in the last hour.

Climbing from my car, I step around the fire engine blocking my way to see a house on fire. It takes me a second to realise whose house it is, and then my feet are moving.

"Get out of the way. Move," I yell as I shove my way through the crowds lining the street. I skid to a halt as I reach the edge of the police cordon, almost ploughing into a copper preventing people from getting closer.

"Hey, hold it there—"

"That's my house. Let me the fuck through now!" Before he can reply or stop me, I duck under his arm and run toward the house, only to be stopped a second later when an arm wraps around my waist, pulling me back.

"Sarge, it's me, Smithy. Stop fighting. You can't go in there." Smithy's voice finally reaches my brain, and I stop struggling. He holds me up as my knees almost give out when I see the smouldering remains of my home.

"Fuck!" The word is exhaled on a harsh breath. There's a loud crash as part of the roof collapses, and dark black smoke billows up, curling around the clouds like a noose. And I can almost feel it as though it were around my own neck.

"I'm sorry, Sarge," Smithy says as I find my feet again.

"I'm not your Sergeant anymore, Smithy. Just plain old Roxy now." He releases me, and I take a step back.

"Nah, you'll always be Sarge to me."

"Thanks, Smithy." I give him a pat on the shoulder as I turn and walk back to my car, ignoring him as he calls after me. I reverse the car back out to the main road and find a place to park while I wait.

Several hours pass by, and as I watch a fire engine pulling out of my road, I start the car and drive back to what's left of my home.

It's not a pretty sight. Black scorch marks climb the wall from every window, and the frames are charred and buckled. The acrid scent of burnt plastic lingers in the air accompanied by little flakes of ash that float down from the sky.

I watch the last of the firemen as they roll their hoses back up and load them on to the fire engine. I see Smithy talking to a fireman, and I walk over to him.

He introduces me, and I'm given a quick run-down on what they believe happened. Petrol bomb apparently. The building isn't safe for me to enter, not that there's anything for me to salvage by the looks of it. As the fireman walks away, I notice my neighbours, a family with two small children, huddled on the side of the road.

"Smithy, do they have somewhere to stay?" He turns to look at where my focus is before turning back to me.

"Yeah, they have a family member they can stay with for now. How about you, you got somewhere you can stay?"

I drag my eyes away from the family and look at Smithy. "I'm good, don't worry about me. But do me a favour, send me the bill for whatever they need, okay."

"Of course. I have to go, but don't be a stranger, Sarge."

Back in my car, I search for an Airbnb close by and manage to find one that I can have tonight even though it's late.

With nothing but what I'm wearing and a boot full of food, I drive toward my temporary home.

Chapter Twelve

Maddox

Sweat glistens across my bare chest, and it heaves with exertion as I watch Axel's eyes roll to the back of his head from the force of the hit Zak just planted on him.

"Are you ready to talk now, Axel?" He spits blood from his mouth, a tooth among the sticky, congealed mess on the floor.

"I can't tell you why. It's more than my life is worth," he slurs, lisping due to the missing front tooth now lying at my feet.

"You have no fucking idea how true those words are." I nod to Zak standing behind him, and he wraps an arm around Axel's neck, squeezing until he turns blue and almost passes out from lack of oxygen. Giving him another nod, Zak releases him. Axel gasps and sucks air into his starved lungs, his head dropping, chin to chest, as his breathing begins to level out.

"Please, Maddox, you know me. You know I'd never betray you."

"Bullshit! I thought I knew you. Thought I could trust you."

"You can trust me, but—" His lies are cut short as my anger takes control, and I pound into his body like a fucking punching bag at the gym. When I'm spent, I turn away from him, unable to see the damage I've done to someone I thought was a friend.

I hear Zak talking to him, trying to get him to give up whatever it is that turned him into the fucking rat bastard he is.

I swipe a towel from the bench and wipe the sweat and blood from my face as my phone pings with a message. Throwing the towel back down, I pick it up and open the message. It's a photo of a burning house, and at first, I miss the figure standing to the side at the forefront. Zooming in to get a better look, features that I recognise emerge.

Roxanne.

"Son of a bitch!" I shove the phone into my back pocket and turn to Zak. "You good with him?"

"Sure. What's going on?"

I don't get a chance to answer as Axel pipes up instead. "Roxy. He'll never stop till he gets what he wants, Maddox. He's gunning for her."

I storm across the basement floor until I'm almost chest to chest with Axel. Taking his chin in my grasp, I lean forward and snarl in his face, "If there's one fucking hair out of place on her head, I'm going to come back here and show you exactly how fucked up I am. Then I'm going to make sure every fucker out there gets to see what happens to rats!" I throw his head back as I release him, and it bounces off the wall with a crack. "Do what you want to the cunt, but I want him alive when I get back. I have something special for this particular traitor."

Any guilt I was feeling about Axel has been eclipsed by my concern for Roxanne. I'm not ready to tell her or fully admit my feelings for her, but I'll be damned if I'll let anything happen to her after we've spent the last ten years of our lives protecting her.

I know Zak feels the same, although we've never really spoken about it. It's always just been there between us, a mutual affection for out feisty little blonde firecracker. I may have buried my guilt at leaving her the way we did and selfishly stealing her first kiss the night everything changed, but it took years and me claiming countless lives before I reached this point.

I watched from afar as she spiralled out of control on a well-worn path of self-destruct while I became a ruthless, no holds barred killer.

There's no better way to exorcise your demons than spilling the blood of your enemies and being buried balls deep in pussy and sky high on a cocktail of drugs.

Only problem with all of that is that every time I pulled that fucking trigger, I pictured someone else's face. Every time I fucked some chick, I wished it were someone else. And every time I got high, her face haunted my mind like a spectre.

I race through town to Roxanne's house with a fire so fierce inside me I can almost feel my blood boiling beneath my skin as it surges through my veins.

When I screech to a stop outside what used to be Roxanne's home and see the shell of what's left, I explode.

Slamming my already battered fists against the steering wheel, the dash and even the window, which breaks into a thousand tiny pieces all of which remain in place.

There's only one person who is sure to know where she is. Hitting dial on my phone, I don't even let him get out a hello.

"Where the fuck is she?" I hear rustling in the background and a door closing before his voice comes back at me.

"I told you to never call me on this number, Lawler."

"I don't give two shits what you told me. Now, where the fuck is she?" I grit my teeth and feel my jaw crack with the force.

"Tucked up in bed if she has any fucking sense," he

mutters, and I hear him rubbing at the day-old stubble on his chin. "What's going on?"

"You better hope she wasn't tucked up in bed seeing as her house is a smouldering pile of fucking ash."

"Fucking hell."

"Yeah, fucking hell. Now find her. Can't you track her on her phone?"

"She's not a damn kid, Lawler. Now, give me two minutes, and I'll call you back." He doesn't wait for a reply before he's hung up.

Agitation eats at me, and I'm just about to call him back when my phone rings.

"About fucking time!"

"She's fine, she's safe. She wasn't home and is staying at an Airbnb for now."

"You got an address?"

"No, I don't, and I wouldn't give it to you if I had." The line goes dead again, and I can't say I blame the guy. I consider calling him back just to piss him off, but I leave him alone. His involvement in all of this is already going to cause some shit.

Instead, I call Bowser as he's always good with this techy crap. "Hey, I need you to track a phone," I say when he answers. It's clear I've disturbed him from his gruff tone, but I don't give two fucks.

I give him Roxanne's number and within five minutes I have a rough vicinity to search for her. It's narrowed down by the number of phone masts in the area but not an exact location.

I drive around the area and get lucky when I spot her car. Eventually, after searching for Airbnb places in this road, I find her.

I could knock, but where's the fun in that, plus I'm kind of fucked off right now, so lock picking it is.

It doesn't take me long to open the front door, and to

anyone watching it would look like I was just fumbling with my key, not that I really give a fuck. The mood I'm in and with the blood still splattered across my knuckles from Axel, you'd have to be certifiably insane to approach me.

I step inside, closing the door behind me. It's a nice place, but she's not staying here. I'm not quiet as I walk through the house, and by the time I reach the top of the stairs, I already know she's heard me. I heard her too.

There's only two bedrooms up here, and the first one is directly opposite the stairs and empty. Turning to the right, I move toward the second bedroom. Pushing the door further open, I step inside.

It's the slightest sound from behind me that gives her away, and as I spin to face her, she swings at me. I duck, side stepping as she comes again. This time, I grab her before she can even swing whatever the fuck it is she's wielding.

"Calm down, Roxanne," I whisper in her ear, and I brush my lips against her neck, unable to resist the lure of her sweet-smelling skin. It's been fucking years since I was this close to her, and it has my body going fucking crazy. Just like the other night in her kitchen and again in my office, my cock is like a fucking steel rod.

I feel the shiver that runs down her body, and I bask in it. But it's broken almost as quick as it came when she stomps her foot down on top of mine, catching the bridge just right, and pain radiates all the way up my calf.

"Calm down! Are you fucking insane?" she yells, pacing back to the bed and putting the small lamp she was holding down. I see some of the fight go out of her and her breathing level out now she knows there's no threat. "What the fuck are you doing here, and how the hell did you find me, Maddox?"

"Get your shit together, you're coming with me," I tell her as I find the light and switch it on.

"Like fuck I am!" she seethes.

When I turn back to her, I'm not prepared for the sight that greets me. If I thought my dick was hard before, now it's fucking granite. She's wearing a black silk babydoll nightie with sheer lace covering her breasts, which does nothing to hide her peaked nipples, that barely reaches the top of her thighs.

I fight back a groan and the need to adjust myself as her reply finally makes it to my lust fogged brain.

"Get dressed, Roxanne, or I'll carry you out as you are. After the shit evening I've had, you don't want to test my fucking patience." I watch her nostrils flare and eyes darken as she stalks toward me.

"Go to hell, Maddox!" she says, spitting the words at me like darts, and I can see she means every single one. She hates me, as well she should, but I know there are other feelings running parallel.

Standing toe to toe, her eyes scan my face, and I see the moment something catches her attention, and I realise there must still be some blood splatters on my face. In the next few seconds, I watch as she wars with her need to check I'm okay and not hurt and her rage at the thought of what I was doing before I arrived here.

"Not my blood, Tinks." She gasps as her nickname falls from my lips so fucking easily, and I love how natural it feels to say it again. The nickname I gave her after she made us watch *Peter Pan* one day, and I realised how much she's like Tinkerbell. I reach out, tracing my thumb over the barely visible scar on her chin, which she received after falling from a swing when she was 14, before gripping it and tilting her face up to mine.

Her eyes are glassy and swirling with emotions as I lean closer to her mouth, almost touching her lips with my own.

"Get dressed before I take you right fucking here and show you who you belong to." I slam my lips to hers, cutting off any retort. Her lips are firm against mine, but slowly they soften, allowing me to slip my tongue inside her warm, sweet mouth and taste a hint of cherries. As desperate as I am to fuck her, I pull away, breaking the kiss and spinning her round.

"Clothes, Roxanne," I say, slapping her on the arse. She lets out a breathy yelp at the sting on her bare skin. "You have ten minutes. I'll be downstairs," I tell her as I leave.

Downstairs, I adjust my rock-hard cock and pace the hallway. I hold back the urge to punch something because this is not how I planned things to go. I shoot a text to Zak to give him a heads up we're going to have a guest. I hear Roxanne coming down the stairs just as his reply comes through, and I'm thankful to see she's wearing clothes. I'm still holding my phone and more than a little tempted to snap a picture of the pissed off look on her face, but I don't and shove my phone back in my pocket.

When she reaches the bottom of the stairs, she doesn't even look at me, instead pushes passed me and heads for the small galley kitchen.

I follow her and lean against the door frame and watch as she begins loading shopping bags with food from the fridge and cupboards.

"What the fuck are you doing?" She ignores me, and I step forward, snatching the bag she's holding from her hand. All patience lost and needing to get the fuck out of here, I drop the bag and pick her up, throwing her over my shoulder.

I march toward the front door, snatching up the small bag she carried downstairs, while Roxanne kicks her feet and slams her fists, which might be small but pack one hell of a punch, into my back. I narrowly miss getting a kick to the nuts as I spot the house keys on a table by the front door and snatch them up. As soon as we step outside, she starts screaming, and I quickly lock up and post the keys through the letterbox. Once my hands are free, I slap her hard on the arse, expecting it to shut her up, but all it does is send a signal to my already straining cock, and when a moan escapes from her, I almost shoot my load in my boxers like a fucking teen. Lights come on over the road, and I catch sight of the curtain twitching as I move down the path to my car.

Yanking the passenger door open, I drop her into the seat and reach over her to grab the seatbelt before clicking it in place.

"I fucking hate you, Maddox Lawler," she says coldly, folding her arms across her chest. I let out a chuckle and give her a wink as I close the door.

Chapter Thirteen

Roxy

I don't speak to the fucker next to me the whole way to wherever the fuck he's taking me. Some clapped-out, half renovated warehouse where all the *gang* live like one big happy fucking family. Obviously, I know that's not true because I've seen the list of properties Maddox and Zak own, and whilst they do own a warehouse, it's not their home or even their base but simply a warehouse. Despite outward appearances, the Lawler brothers are an entity all by themselves. They have people that work for them, sure, but they don't operate the same way as many of the other criminal organisations do, and they aren't affiliated with any other gangs. Not like they were before.

Even if I wanted to speak to Maddox, I'm not sure I could. I'm still reeling from that kiss. It had my toes curling into the rich, thick carpet and butterflies flitting through my belly. His threat alone had my clit throbbing and my nipples as hard as diamonds. The thought makes me shift in my seat and combined with the tense atmosphere and heat inside the car, I need some air. Rolling down the window, I breath in the cold, fresh air, and it's like a salve to my heated skin.

I can feel Maddox's eye on me as I fiddle with the strap of my handbag, which I managed to keep hold of as he carried me out of the house, but I keep my face firmly turned away from him.

I hate him. And I hate Zak. The two of them broke me in a way I never knew you could be broken at a time I didn't think I could possibly be broken any more than I already was.

I close my eyes, and I'm transported back to that night. To me in the back of that ambulance after just witnessing my mother's dead body being wheeled away, my phone nestled in my hands as I hit dial on Maddox's name again. I bring it to my ear only to be instantly greeted by his voicemail this time. I try Zak again, and all the while I'm begging him to pick up, but he doesn't.

I tried ringing them every day, multiple times, for a solid week after that night with no response. Then as if they never existed, their numbers stopped working, and they're voicemails were replaced with 'this number is no longer in service'.

For the next three months, I was wild. Partying all night, most days too, getting arrested for minor offences and shipped from care home to care home. I was lost, broken and alone.

Thank God for Mitch. Without him, I'd be locked up or dead.

I'm brought back to now by the sound of metal clanking against metal, and I open my eyes to see a pair of black ornate metal gates swinging open in front of me. Add a backdrop of fire and I could almost be entering the Gates of Hell.

I can see the house up ahead, and as we approach, the front door opens and out steps Zak along with a guy I don't recognise.

They talk on the front steps of the double fronted Victorian house while Maddox parks in the garage alongside a dark coloured Alfa Romeo and a matte black motorbike with a metallic gold engine and forks.

Maddox climbs from the car and waits for me, but when I don't move, he steps to my side, opening the door.

"Out of the car, Roxanne." Still refusing to look at him and despite feeling like a petulant child, I remain where I am. "Fuck's sake. I don't have time for this childish shit," he grumbles, reaching inside the car, unclipping my seatbelt and picking me up. I do absolutely nothing to help, instead making sure I'm as relaxed as possible so that he's carrying my dead weight.

He passes right by Zak and the guy he's talking to without so much as a hello, walking straight inside and up the stairs.

When he reaches his destination, he shoves through the door and unceremoniously dumps me on the bed before turning around and walking out.

"Sleep well, Roxanne," he calls as he disappears down the hall.

I almost shout out a 'fuck you' but hold it back after his words to me the last time I said it. I don't need to be turned on any more than I already am, especially when I should want to kill him and Zak not get down and dirty with them—him. Jeez, I don't even know which way is up right now. I'm exhausted.

Without turning on the light and after closing the door, I discover that there's an en suite and quickly relieve myself and change out of my clothes for the second time tonight.

Crawling under the heavy, yet soft, duvet, which is no doubt feather, I sprawl out like a starfish in the queen-sized bed. Partly because I can and partly because I need to keep my hands away from my needy and traitorous vagina. There is no way I'm getting myself off to thoughts of Maddox's kiss or his hard length I felt pressing up against me earlier tonight.

No fucking way.

I failed miserably last night having woken sometime early this morning with my hand inside my knickers and fingers working my clit in rough circles while using my other hand to twist and pull at my beaded nipples and bringing myself to orgasm.

I struggled to go back to sleep after that despite my orgasm and having had barely any sleep. I now find myself pacing up and down the room and procrastinating about whether I'm ready to go downstairs and face Maddox and Zak or just stay here indefinitely.

I'm not enjoying the chaotic and adverse emotions they are drawing out of me. I don't know what to do with these feelings or how to protect myself from once again being that heart broken and lonely seventeen-year-old. I don't know if I have the strength to stop myself from falling down the rabbit hole of self-destruct.

I always knew that allowing them back into my life would be hard, but I never expected for all those feelings, good and bad, from years ago to have such a conflicting impact on me. I'm scared of who I'll become if I let them close. I'm scared that I'll lose the core of who I am; morally just, loyal, fierce but good hearted.

I know deep down there's another side to me, one that goes against every fibre of the person standing here right now. But she's there, clawing to get free, and all it would take is one tiny fracture in her carefully constructed cage for her to burst free and bring a wrath so fierce and violent it would be apocalyptic.

Needing something to take my mind off where I am and the two men sure to ruin me, I make some calls. An hour later, I've spoken to my house insurance company and my gas, electricity and water suppliers, and I've also spoken to Smithy, who called to check on me and promised to let me know as soon as he hears back from the fire department.

Feeling like I've shored up my walls enough and in desperate need of coffee, food and some new clothes, in that order, I head downstairs.

It's still early, and I don't know if the house being quiet means everyone is still asleep or if they're not here. Guess I'm about to find out.

After a quick check of all the rooms and deduce there's no one here, I head to the kitchen. I make a coffee using the fancy machine they have, and find some crumpets, which I shove in the toaster.

I make light work of the coffee and crumpets and am just loading my dirty cup and plate into the dishwasher when I feel someone watching me.

A quick glance out the corner of my eye, and I know it's Zak. Bending down to place the butter knife I used in the cutlery holder, it slips from my hand, hitting the floor and spinning away from me.

"Fuck," I mutter, before standing upright and turning around. Zak is standing right in front of me holding the butter knife out to me and wearing a pair of suit trousers and a shirt, unbuttoned and displaying his tatted and toned abs.

Lord have fucking mercy.

"Morning, Rox," he says as I take the knife. "Did you sleep well?"

I snort at his fucking dumb arse question. "No, surprisingly not." I drop the knife into the cutlery holder and close the dishwasher. Pulling my phone from my pocket, I'm just ordering an Uber when Maddox stalks into the room. When my eyes lift to take him in, he's wearing even less than Zak, and my tongue about falls out of my mouth and hits the floor.

Unable to talk while I metaphorically roll up my tongue, Maddox walks past me to the coffee machine.

"You won't need an Uber," he states, and I spin to face him.

"Ignoring the fact that it's rude to read over someone's shoulder, why don't I need an Uber?"

"Because your car is out the front." I glare at him, trying to make out the lie, but there isn't one. Turning, I begin walking to the front door when Maddox's voice carries down the hall to me.

"But you also aren't going anywhere, so it doesn't really matter." I stop unsure I heard him correctly when he speaks again, "It's not safe, so whatever it is you need, you can get delivered or one of us will collect it for you."

I slowly pace back to the kitchen, all the while my mind fighting with which part of what he just said I want to question first.

"I'm sorry, but I'm almost certain you just told me I can't go out like I'm a grounded teenager. But that can't be right because I'm a grown arse fucking woman who can and will do whatever the fuck I want when I want. And I'll be damned if I let you or anybody else"—I turn my fury towards Zak for a fraction of a second before glaring back at Maddox—"tell me what to do, Maddox-almighty-fucking-Lawler. So, let's try this again. I say, 'somebody burnt my house down, so I need to go shopping', at which point you say, 'have a nice time, Roxy'. Simple."

"I'm certain there should be a curse in there somewhere, Rox, and Mad would never say 'have a nice time' like he has roses blooming from his arse," Zak says, a humorous smirk curling one side of his mouth.

Although I appreciate him trying to make light of Maddox's caveman act, it doesn't deter from the fact Maddox thinks he can tell me what to do like I'm a piece of fucking property.

Maddox turns his icy glare to Zak. "Not helping, man."

"Look, thanks for letting me stay last night, but I can't be here. Aside from the fact I'm meant to be laying low, it's wrong."

"What the fuck does that mean, Roxanne?"

"It means, I may no longer be a cop, but how do you think it will look if I'm suddenly holed up with two of London's most notorious criminals?"

"I don't give a shit how it looks. You being here is what needs to happen, end of story."

"No, Maddox, not end of story. In fact, you haven't even given me the prologue, instead I've been dropped into this fucking shit storm in *medias res*. This is not some fucking novel; this is my life. A life I worked hard for and have had to throw away because of you. So, excuse me if I'm a bit put out, although royally pissed better describes how I feel right now. I've lost my job and my house, and now you just expect me to move in here with you two? I don't fucking think so. Unless you can give me a damn good reason, then it ain't happening." I spin on my heels and storm from the house without even taking a breath.

When I reach my car, which is as Maddox said parked out front, I realise my mistake.

No fucking keys.

Chapter Fourteen

Zak

The front door slams shut as Maddox slams his fist down on the kitchen counter, cursing like a sailor.

"Mad—"

"Don't, Zak, just go with her. I have some things I need to deal with here." He throws Roxy's car keys to me, which I catch, before I turn and leave him to it.

I run upstairs to grab a jacket and my phone before heading out. I've just finished buttoning my shirt as I step outside and see Rox kick the tyre of her car before striding off down the drive to the gates.

I pull up next to her as she stands there looking for a button to open the gates, but she won't find one. I wind down the window and push the gate fob in my pocket as she turns to me.

"Oh, hell no," she says, waving her hand and shaking her head.

"Come on, Rox." I step out of the car and walk to the passenger side. "I'll even let you drive," I say, giving her a wink. The fact I'm offering to let her drive her own car amuses me, and her too given the half smile she tries to hide.

"This is bullshit, Zak. Bullshit." She climbs behind the wheel, pulling her seatbelt across her body and snapping it into place before driving out onto the main road.

She's quiet and clearly on edge as we drive into town, and I allow her the time knowing this must be hard for her.

She parks just outside Oxford Circus, and we walk down to Oxford Street, weaving in and out of the Sunday morning crowds, which are mainly tourists.

I'm not surprised she picked here, knowing that it's a neutral territory when it comes to gangs and most crime here is from opportunist pickpockets.

I hang back while she flits in and out of shops, purchasing items as though she's reading from a list. When she slips inside the next shop, I almost groan.

Stepping inside behind her, the assistant approaches her instantly and asking if she requires any help, Rox shakes her head and walks away. As I go to follow, the assistant asks me the same thing, her eyes taking me in from head to toe, and I hear the double meaning behind her question and see the desire in her eyes.

I walk away without replying and catch up to Rox as she scans through a rail of matching bra and knicker sets, picking a few before moving on to nightwear.

When she picks a couple and heads to the changing room, I come up with some inventive ways to murder Maddox for this.

My suit trousers are suddenly feeling very fucking tight as she hands me the underwear to hold while she tries sexy as fuck negligees on behind a flimsy curtain.

While I wait, I take a look in the sex toys section. It does fuck all to ease the uncomfortable situation going on in my trousers, and when Rox sidles up beside me, taking back the underwear she handed me, and picks up a box containing a small three-pronged clitoral vibrator and a rose-gold bullet, I fucking growl.

"Did you just growl?" she asks, with a cocked brow and a smirk.

Stepping into her and leaning down, I whisper, "Fuck, yeah, I did, Rox. Are you trying to fucking kill me? I know you're pissed with us, but this is plain torture."

"A girl needs a little relief every now and again. This is only scraping the surface of what I had in my collection before my house burned to the ground, Zak."

I push against her back, forcing her forward until she's flat against the wall. "You know, I have my own collection." I grind my hips, making sure she feels how turned on I am, then spin away from her, leaving her breathless.

I wait outside for her, sending a message to Maddox telling him what an arsehole he is. His reply consists of the middle finger emoji.

When she finally emerges, she looks flushed, and my mind conjures an image of her back in the changing room pleasuring herself. Fuck! I need to get my shit together. I'm certain Maddox didn't have this in mind when he sent me after her. Or maybe he did as payback for the shit that went down between them last night.

With my hand at her back, I begin leading her away. "Is there anything else you need?" Before she can reply, a guy walking past knocks into her, causing her to drop her bags.

"Watch it, arsehole" I call after him, and he turns to face me, recognition flaring as he swipes a hand across his neck with a laugh before disappearing into the crowd. "Shit," I mutter, bending to help Rox pick up her bags. "Come on, let's get out of here," I say, hurrying Rox back down the street to where her car is parked, and scanning the crowd as we go.

"Zak, hold up, I still need some things. What's the rush?"

"Whatever else you need, I'll get for you."

"No, Zak—" she begins, but I cut her off, pulling on her arm and causing her to come to a stop.

"Look around you, Rox. What do you see?" I watch as she turns her eyes to the people passing by, the groups on the corners chatting to each other or on their phones, then I see the moment she spots them.

Nestled among the crowds are several members of Bonner's crew, distinctive due to the blue bandannas hanging from their back left pockets. As if they know we are watching them, their gazes seek us out.

"What the hell are they doing here?" she asks, looking back to me.

"Let's not hang around to find out." I take half the bags from her hands, slipping my free hand into hers, and head for the car.

Back at the house, I set Rox up with my laptop so she can order whatever we didn't manage to get in town, and I head to the office to call Maddox.

When he doesn't answer, I decide to pay our other guest a visit. I check that Rox is busy before disappearing downstairs.

The house had a huge cellar when we purchased it, and it didn't take much to convert it to what we needed. We divided it into two rooms and put in a small shower room, for obvious reasons. Generally, we try not to bring our work home with us now, but needs must sometimes. Since we parted ways with Theo, a lot has changed.

I find Axel slumped in the corner of the first room, wearing nothing but his boxers, and the stench of piss stings my nostrils. The metallic scent of blood isn't even enough to overpower it despite it coating the floor like paint.

He groans as my foot meets his leg, and he peels a swollen eye lid open.

"Zak...please, man."

"No point begging, rat. You had your chance. I'm surprised Maddox hasn't already finished you off and sent you back to Bonner in a box all tied up with a nice little fucking bow." I grab one of the chairs, swinging it round and sitting down, arms leaning on the back.

"You don't...understand. I...fuck," he says as he shifts his body into a more upright position. "It's not what you think." His face screws up tight from the pain of moving.

"You know, I've heard that line so many times, I swear it's etched on my brain. Anyway, what I came down here for is some information. And I think you at least owe us that much while you've still got a tongue in your head." Axel shakes his head, but before he can say anything, I continue, "Where's Tommy?"

He frowns. "I don't know, Zak. I swear."

I nod as though agreeing with him. "Really? But I thought you, Rogers, and Bonner were best buddies, that's why you're here knocking at death's door, right?"

"It's not like—" He breaks off, hacking up a lung. "It's not like that."

I reach down, sliding up the leg of my trousers and pull a small blade from its holster. "I think we should try this again. Where is Tommy?" I ask, rising from the chair and tossing it across the room. "I'm a patient man, Axel, but I'm sure you already know what happens when that extensive patience wears out," I tell him, crouching down in front of him, gripping his chin and turning his face to me. "Where the fuck is Tommy?" I bring the blade up so it's pointing directly at the one eye he can open and close enough it's the only thing he can see.

"I don't know. As far as I know, he left town after Maddox

put the word out on him." He coughs again, halting when he realises the movement is bringing my blade ever closer to piercing his eyeball.

"See, I kind of thought that too, but the funny thing is when I was in Oxford Street earlier today, I saw him. And that wouldn't normally be a problem, but he wasn't alone. Do you have any idea who he might have been with, Axel?" He shakes his head minutely, and I move the blade an inch closer, ensuring he understands what happens if he's lying to me. "You sure about that? 'Cause I think you're lying to me, Axel, and I don't like fucking liars anytime, but especially when people I care about are in danger."

I watch as he finally realises that I'm not fucking around with this. I'm surprised it took him so long. He knows me, knows what I'm capable of, and what Theo discovered my talent is. It seems there is place for art in the world of organised crime, especially when my medium of choice is the sharp edge of a blade.

His eyes widen as I touch the blade just below his eye, slowly sliding it down his face, over his chin and stopping at the pulse point beating away in his neck.

"If I was to make a small puncture mark just here and hang you upside down, do you know how long it would take for you to bleed out?"

"N-n-no," he stutters, swallowing hard.

"Me neither, but how about we find out?" I grip one of his ankles and give a small tug, and he lets out a groan that turns to a scream as I tug harder, dragging him across the floor.

"Fuck! Stop, stop, okay. He's joined up with Bonner," he shouts, finishing on a cry as I drop his leg to the floor. He collapses, dropping his head back and breathing heavily.

"No fucking shit!" I move over him, a leg either side of his torso, and bend down, pressing the tip of my blade to his sternum. Feeling the cold tip against his skin, he opens his one eye, fear shining bright. I push a little harder into his skin, and a bead of blood blooms to the surface causing the corner of my lip to curve in a wicked smile. When I begin carving into his skin, he screams, and his hands reach out, gripping my wrist to stop me, but I pin them above his head with my other hand before going back to my art. Painting my pain all over my target like a fucking artist. I feel the first stirring of pleasure swirl in my gut as I finish the first letter. I continue, and all the while, the image of Roxy sitting in that ambulance heartbroken, tears tracking down her face, as she hits redial again and again flashes through my mind.

I push away thoughts of what she would think of me if she saw me now, if she knew the things I had done and instead focus on the end game. I'm so lost to what I'm doing that I don't hear the shuffling of feet against the cold, hard concrete, or the sound of someone calling my name. I can't even hear Axel's screams as I carve the final line.

A hand on my shoulder, startles me, and I spin round, blade raised ready to strike.

"Enough, Zak," he says, as I step away from Axel laid out beneath me, the word rat barely visible through the pools of blood spilling down the sides of his torso. "Go and get cleaned up," he tells me as he leans down, whispering something I can't hear to Axel.

I clean up in the small shower room, watching the water turn pink and trying my best to ignore the fact I'm hard and would normally find someone, usually Lila, to help relieve me right about now.

But I don't think Lila would cut it this time as an image of Rox in one of the sexy as fuck skimpy bra and knicker sets she purchased earlier pops into my head. Knowing there's no chance of that happening, I take myself in my hand, squeezing tight before slowly sliding my hands up and down my slick shaft. Resting my head on the wall, water dripping over my head and down my body, I speed up as my balls tighten, picturing Rox's mouth around my cock as I thrust in and out, groaning out my release and shooting streams of cum up the tiles.

Back in my room, I forgo my usual shirt and suit trousers and find a pair of joggers and a tee to throw on instead. I'm lying on my bed with my eyes closed, wracking my brains about why Axel would fucking switch on us. What the hell is he protecting? Then I remember the girl from his flat, Eva Trent. I'm just about to get up and check out her address when there's a knock on my door.

Chapter Fifteen

Roxy

I knock on Zak's door, pushing it open before he can reply and step inside. I'm surprised to find him sprawled out on his bed wearing something other than a suit. It's a nice surprise, especially the glimpse of his toned abs, which are covered in tatts, where his t-shirt has ridden up. I quickly look away, not wanting him to catch me eye fucking him.

"Hey, sorry. I just wanted to return this to you. Thanks," I say, stepping forward and holding it out to him. I can't read his face at all. It's like he's pulled a shutter down as soon as I walked into the room. He doesn't make any move to take the laptop from me or say anything. "I tried to find you earlier. Where did you disappear off to?" I ask the question casually, but it doesn't matter what answer he gives me because I already know the answer.

"I had some business to deal with. Did you get everything you need?" He finally gets up, taking the laptop from my hand, his fingertips brushing mine.

"Yeah, I did. This *business* of yours, wouldn't have anything to do with the guy you were torturing down in the cellar, would it?" His head snaps up, eyes locking with mine.

"You forget what I did for a living, Zak?" He stares at me for a couple more seconds before turning away and placing the laptop on a desk along the back wall.

"Nah, I didn't forget, Rox. You don't seem surprised?" he asks, keeping his back to me.

I step a little closer. "I'm not. I didn't forget what you do or who you are, Zak. Doesn't mean I have to like it." What he doesn't know and what I'm ashamed to admit is that watching him today, seeing him causing pain to someone that hurt him and Maddox, turned me on. I should be disgusted with myself. It goes against everything a cop should stand for, everything I stand for and have been taught. It's not how you get justice, not in my world.

He spins around, and I see fury in his eyes, and something else that I'm not quite sure of. "I don't need you to like it. It is what it is. You do your job, and I'll do mine."

And now it's my turn feel the flames of fury lick up my skin as I fold my arms across my body. "Really? And what is my job, huh? Because so far, all the two of you have done is barge your way back into my life and fucking ruin it, Zak." His wince is so slight that had I blinked I'd have missed it, but I don't miss his sigh.

"You can be pissed all you want, but you had a choice."

"A choice? Blackmail doesn't come with choices, Zak. It comes with bad or fucked. There was no option that didn't end my career, my life. One I worked fucking hard to achieve, and you fucking know it. So, don't give me some bullshit about choice." I wave my hand dismissively at him.

"You didn't have to quit, Rox. That's not what we asked of you."

"Do you honestly believe that I would have compromised my integrity, dishonoured all my hard work by staying on the job only for you and your brother to bring it all down around me? You're fucking delusional if you do. And it shows how little you know me, but then that's not surprising is it?"

"Yet, you were happy enough to discredit yourself. For what, Rox? Your integrity?"

"Yes, actually. I'd rather burn down my own career than give you and Maddox the satisfaction of destroying me a second time." The words burn on the way out because they're a lie. They will destroy me again, and it seems that I'm prepared to let them. What a fucking joke. But one thing I do know is that I won't go down easy.

Zak sighs, and there's a small spark of remorse on his face for a fraction of a second. "I get it, you're pissed, you don't trust us, and I don't blame you. You'll get your answers, but for now, you just need to do as Maddox asks. I know how hard that is for you." There's humour in his voice, and I see the twitch of his lips as he tries to hold back a smile. "That's something that hasn't changed," he adds a little forlornly.

I know that if I ask the next obvious questions—where the fuck were you? Why did you leave me? I'm going to be forced to face a truth I'm just not sure I'm completely ready for. While I've been contemplating my response, Zak has picked a pair of trousers and a shirt from his wardrobe.

It seems my moment to ask has passed for now as he disappears into the en-suite and emerges two minutes later dressed much as he was this morning, except his shirt is buttoned this time. He grabs socks from his chest of drawers and sits on the edge of the bed to put them on.

His clothing style is such a damn contradiction, and nothing like he wore when we were kids. But I guess back then he didn't have the money, none of us did.

The air is thick with so many things unsaid that the next words from my lips make me cringe internally, and I mentally slap myself as they leave my mouth.

"Hot date?"

He rises from where he's sitting, stepping toward me and stopping a mere breath from my face, which due to the significant height difference has me looking at his muscular chest and shoulders. I have to crane my neck to look at his face, and when I do, he's wearing a smirk.

"And if it was?" He leans down, his breath hot against my neck as he whispers, "Would you be jealous, Rox?" His voice is almost a rasp as it rumbles up his throat and vibrates across my ear.

"Would you want me to be," I reply, turning my face a fraction so that my lips are almost touching his cheek. And the word vomit just keeps fucking coming. Why can't I seem to control my emotions or my body around him? Earlier in the shop, I had to contain the need to strip there and then and get myself off, and I was still flushed when I finally grew a pair and stepped outside. I don't think I've ever felt so bloody shy, embarrassed, unsettled around anybody in my entire life. I'm not usually so easily rattled, and it freaks me the fuck out. Everything about this whole situation was a bad idea from the outset. I knew it then and I know it now, so why didn't I tell them to fuck off and do their worst? Surely, nothing could be as bad as this right now.

He chuckles in my ear, and I jump as his hands grip my waist, pulling my hips toward him as he slips his leg between mine. "I'm not a man you should tease, Rox." He pulls his face back, locking eyes with me, and I go to speak, but his finger on my lips stops me. "Be very careful of your next words because your body doesn't lie, and I can feel the heat from your pussy and beat of your heart." As if to prove his point, he uses his grip on my hips to keep me in place as he rubs his thigh against my core. The friction it creates through the thin material of my joggers forces a moan from me, making my lips part, and he doesn't miss the opportunity to slip his finger between them. I'm lost to the feel of his muscular thigh between my legs and the roughness of his finger as my tongue involuntarily swirls around the tip.

A short cough behind me snaps me out of the lusty haze Zak's managed to pull me into, and I push away from him. He releases me, and I stumble back a step, knocking into a hard wall of muscle. I spin around and come face to face with Maddox who has his arms folded across his chest and a pissed off scowl on his face.

He raises an eyebrow to Zak over my shoulder before his eyes come back to me.

"Get dressed. You're coming with me."

"Er...yeah, hard pass," I say, finally finding my voice and trying to step around him, but it's like trying to sidestep Everest.

I feel heat at my back a second before Zak whispers, "Be a good girl, Rox." His hand brushes over my arse as he steps past and disappears downstairs, and I mentally curse the fucker for leaving me here, somewhat vulnerable, to deal with the pissed of man mountain in front of me.

I go to move around Maddox again, but he blocks me, going a step further as a meaty hand slams against the wall that's now behind me.

"Don't push me, Roxanne. I need to be somewhere, and you're coming with me."

All the anger and hate I feel for him and Zak eclipses the buzz from moments ago. "Listen up, and real good this time. I don't take orders from you or anyone else, and I'm certainly not going anywhere with you until you give me some answers. Got it, big guy? Now move the fuck out of my way. Please," I say with a hyperbolic grin.

His eyes darken, boring into mine, then in the blink of an eye, his hands are on my face and his lips slamming down on mine. I'm so taken aback that for a split second I don't do anything. As the shock wears off, I begin to fight, but it only makes him hold me tighter and kiss me harder. When he pushes me into the wall, I feel how turned on he his, and I lose the battle, giving in to my body's demands. I part my lips, finally allowing him entry, and hitch my leg up over his hip so I can get the friction I so desperately need. Between Zak before and now Maddox, I'm going to need some relief.

I can taste notes of whiskey and smoke as our tongues battle, and as he grinds his hips, he swallows the moan I can no longer contain as I submit to him.

Then it's gone. His lips on mine, the heat of his body and his hands on my face, all just disappear as quick as it started. I open my eyes, breathless and dizzy from his intoxicating taste, to see him with a devilish smirk curling at his lips and hazel eyes swirling like molten gold.

I'm unable to look away as his tongue swipes across his bottom lip, and I see his satisfaction at how easy he was able to break me.

"Get dressed," he orders, then turns and walks away leaving me unsatisfied and so fucking angry. With him but more so with myself.

I slam the bedroom door, then open it and slam it again just in case he didn't get the message on how pissed off I am the first time. Childish? Sure. Satisfying? A little.

If Maddox Lawler wants to play games, then let's fucking play. I have no idea where we're going, and I don't exactly have a full wardrobe to choose from, but I did pick up some nice jeans and a couple of tops that will work.

Quickly changing, I even find some mascara, eyeliner and lipstick in my handbag. I'm not big on the makeup front, so these basics will do just fine.

I consider why I'm even doing this as I put some slap on my face with my limited supplies. It's not like I owe them anything. But equally, I didn't agree because I wanted to help them either.

I don't understand my conflicting feelings toward them. I should hate them, and I do, but there's more than that too. How else can I explain my attraction to them? I never understood then, and now it's even more impossible to wrap my head around. After all this time, after they abandoned me, I should feel nothing, not even hate because they aren't worth the energy it takes.

Finished with my makeup, I'm just checking my reflection in the full-length mirror on the inside of the wardrobe door when the bedroom door flies open.

"Let's go, Roxanne," he demands, standing there dressed from head to toe in black; black jeans, hugging his thick thighs, and black tee, pulled taut across his chest. Tattoos decorate one arm, down to the rose on his right hand.

"Ever heard of knocking, arsehole?" I say, shoving my phone in my back pocket and stifling a laugh and shaking my head at the fact we are dressed identically.

He doesn't reply, just throws a leather jacket at me, which I catch, before simply walking away. I roll my eyes behind his back as I follow. Shoving the jacket on, I breath in the new leather smell and frown when I realise it fits me perfectly.

When we get out to the garage, I walk toward his car but am surprised when he heads for the bike, which I'm now guessing is his and explains the leather jacket.

He passes me a black helmet, and as I turn it, I see a white skull with a bandanna covering the lower half of its face and below it on one side is a sniper rifle while on the other side is some sort of knife and the words Lawless scrawled below.

"Put it on," he says, his words slightly muffled, and when I look at him, I see he already has his on. He throws a leg over the bike, starting it up, and the sound rumbles through the garage.

I shove the helmet on my head and am immediately assaulted by the scent of cedar and smoke, and I realise that this is Maddox's helmet. Pushing my thoughts to the back of my mind, I put my phone in one of the pockets of the jacket that zips up and climb on behind Maddox.

It's not my first time on a motorbike, in fact I dated a guy in college that rode one. Little sparks of excitement thrum through me as the vibrations from the engine revving ripple through my legs and up my body. However, when they reach the apex of my thighs, I realise what hell this is going to be as my earlier arousal returns at Mach speed.

"Oh, fuck!" I mumble, my words drowned out by the engine, or at least so I thought.

"Something the matter, Roxanne?" Maddox's voice rasps in my ear, followed by a deep chuckle.

"Just fucking go, Maddox," I snap, my irritation bleeding through.

"Whatever you say," he replies as he manoeuvres the motorbike out of the garage. "Hold on, Roxanne," he says with a laugh, pulling back on the throttle.

I just manage to wrap my arms around his waist, gripping his leather jacket before we speed down the driveway, kicking up a cloud of dust.

"Motherfucker!" I shout, and my curse is met by more laughter as we hit the road, and my grip tightens on his jacket.

He weaves in and out of traffic expertly, and despite the speed, I feel safe. In no time at all, we pull up to a warehouse set back from the docks, where there's another guy leaning against a bike.

I climb off slowly ensuring I can trust my legs to hold me up and desperately try to ignore the ache between my thighs. I'm so fucking mad with Maddox for a thousand different reasons, and I have a locked chest full of questions in my mind that I plan on asking him, but getting those answers petrifies me.

Starting simple, I ask, "What is this place?" He climbs off

the motorbike, dropping his helmet on the handlebars and holding out his hand for mine, which I just removed. Giving it to him, I wait for him to answer.

He steps up beside me, threading his fingers through mine, and I try to pull away, wondering what the hell he's playing at.

"You have questions and starting now is how you get them. Follow my lead and keep your mouth shut." He tows me toward the other guy, who stands as we approach and reveals his true height.

"What the fuck are you doing, Maddox?" I say through gritted teeth and squeezing his fingers between my own, but there's no time to reply as we come to a stop in front of the guy, who I now recognise as the guy from the pictures Noah showed me the other day.

"Lawler. No Zak tonight, but I see you brought some-thing much more interesting," he says in a lilting Irish brogue. His eyes glide over my body, making my skin crawl with the way he licks his lips, and his eyes light with something dark.

"Aiden, this is Roxanne," Maddox introduces me, pulling me closer to his body.

"Well, well, would you look at that. Who'd a thought that little Detective Sergeant Whitmore would switch sides and become a Lawler whore. Maybe the apple doesn't fall far from the tree after all." He reaches out to me, and I feel Maddox tense beside me, but before his fingertips can touch my face, I turn away, stepping back out of reach.

"Don't touch what you can't afford?" I tell him, and Maddox tenses again.

"Oh, I'm sure I can afford a used up old whore cop. What say you, Lawler? Be sure to pass her over when you're done with her, and I'll show her exactly what money can buy you."

"Sorry, Aiden, was it?" he nods, a confused frown creasing his brow. "That's a good Irish name, and for most, I'm sure they fall at your feet with your Irish brogue to match, but not me I'm afraid. From the moment you opened your mouth, my pussy clamped shut so tight you'd find it easier to thread cotton through the eye of a needle. Go find yourself another whore 'cause you're shit out of luck with this one." I see the hit coming and duck, but I needn't have bothered. When I stand up again, Maddox has Aiden's fist in his hand, shoving it back at him.

"I'm here for business, and my whore is not on the docket," Maddox snarls, and Aiden's eyes narrow before falling to me, his lip curling up in a nasty sneer. "Let's go, Kavanagh, before I change my mind."

Aiden goes first, walking toward the warehouse, but before I can take a step, Maddox grips me hard around the waist, pinning me to his chest with his other hand on my throat.

"I fucking told you to keep your mouth shut." His lips meet mine in a quick but fierce kiss, his hold on my throat tightening a fraction, then as if nothing happened, he releases me, grabs my hand again and begins walking to the warehouse where Aiden disappeared.

I have to skip a little to keep up with his long-arse strides. "You kiss all your *whores* like that?" I try to hide my bitterness at the idea Maddox has a lot of whores, but I fail.

"No, Roxy, just the ones who can't keep their mouths shut and do as they're told." He pauses, and I think he's done. "I usually have them on their knees and choking on my dick no matter where we are, but there's no way in hell Kavanagh is going to see you on your knees. Because when it happens, the only person watching you swallow my cock, will be me."

My breath catches in my throat at the same time I miss a step and almost face plant the ground. Maddox's grip holds me on my feet, and I hear his deep chuckle as we enter the warehouse.

Chapter Sixteen

Maddox

I knew she'd never be able to keep her mouth shut, and it turns me the fuck on listening to her busting Aiden's balls, evidenced by the raging hard on I'm now sporting. Who the fuck am I trying to kid? It's been like a fucking steel rod since I caught her and Zak, but now really isn't the fucking time. Guess that's my own fault for dragging her along with no clue as to what we're doing, where we were going and who we were meeting with.

I wasn't joking about having her on her knees choking on my cock, but for now, kissing her seems to have shut her up. Temporarily.

When she sees what's in the warehouse, kissing her won't do shit to stop the fury coming my way. I just hope she's smart enough to save it till we are somewhere there aren't a dozen eyes and ears and the second in command of the biggest Irish crime family within hearing distance.

As we step inside the warehouse, an icy wind whips around my legs through the open double doors, and I feel Roxanne shiver next to me. I watch as she uses her free hand to pull the sides of her open jacket closer together, trying to keep the chill out.

Roxanne's eyes scan the inside of the warehouse, taking in every little detail like I knew she would. She doesn't miss shit. Her reputation is—was—solid and practically unrivalled on the streets of London. The fact it's marred by her little stunt is a blessing and a damn curse.

My thoughts are cut off as we round the corner and are met by half a dozen of Kavanagh's men all armed and standing guard over the shipment I'm here to purchase.

"Don't mind them," Kavanagh says, turning to face us as we come to a stop in front of a lone crate.

He gives a nod to one of his men, who steps forward to open the crate. I step forward to take a look.

"I've no doubt this will be above and beyond the usual shit you peddle. It's top-notch Columbian cocaine. Pure, not cut with anything else and will blow your fucking mind. You'll party and fuck all night long once it hits your brain."

I don't miss the way his eyes flick to Roxanne when he says it. Neither does she but wisely keeps her mouth shut whilst digging her fingernails into the soft flesh of my hand where it grips hers.

Another guy steps forward, this one a mean motherfucker with a shaved head and a scar that runs the length of one side of his face from temple to chin. His eyes run the length of Roxanne, and he smiles, displaying a mouthful of gold teeth.

I know who he is, Paddy Nolan, aka Knasher. The nickname doesn't require any explanation, especially not when you know his reputation. Known for his brutal underground bareknuckle fighting, often to the death, the gold teeth are replacements for every tooth he's lost during a fight, but he also makes Mike Tyson's nibble of Evander Holyfield's ear look like bedroom foreplay.

He carries a small tray with a tiny metal pipe and pre-cut

lines of coke, placing it on top of another crate beside Kavanagh.

"Come and give your goods a try, Lawler. Or maybe your whore can try some and show us all a good time. Ain't nothing like the buzz of fucking while high, not unless you throw in satisfying your blood lust too. Hell, you could even do it at the same time." He lets out a maniacal laugh, and I don't doubt he's talking from experience given his dilated pupils and the look of glee on his face. Crazy motherfucker.

He turns and picks up the small pipe, holding it out to me and raising his brows in invitation. Knowing this is going to cause fucking hell with Roxanne but having no other choice, I take a step forward. My grip tightens even more on her hand, and I feel an initial tug of resistance before she follows behind me.

Taking the pipe from Kavanagh, and not even daring to look behind me at Roxanne, I release her hand and immediately feel her fingers slip into the back pocket of my jeans, gripping tight, before I lean down to snort a line from the tray.

Throwing the pipe back on the table, I use my thumb to wipe away any residual powder and step back from the crate, taking Roxanne's hand back in mine. Within two minutes, the buzz has kicked in, and I can feel my heart racing inside my chest as a warm glow spreads through my body. Numbness tingles at the back of my nasal passage and throat, making me feel like I can't swallow. Kavanagh wasn't wrong about it being good. I feel fucking wired.

"It's good shit, right? Now let's get down to business."

I give him a nod before I pull my phone from my jacket and send a message to Bowser to bring the cash. A couple of minutes later, a vehicle pulls up outside followed by the thud of a door slamming shut.

Two of Kavanagh's guys move past us, stepping round the

corner into the aisle where I can hear Bowser as he heads this way.

"Easy, fellows, just bringing the cash," he says as the two guys raise their guns at him. When he steps round to meet us, his eyes widen at seeing Roxanne, but he quickly masks his surprise.

Bowser hands me the holdall. "Thanks, man," I say, slapping him on the shoulder as he takes up position next to Roxanne so she's sandwiched between the two of us.

I drop the bag at Kavanagh's feet, and he quickly has a guy come to check it. He crouches, opening the bag and lifting a few wads to check they're legit before giving a nod to Kavanagh.

As soon as the money is exchanged, Bowser brings the van in, and him and Rocky load the crates into it. Once all the goods are loaded, Bowser and Rocky head out to stash it at a new warehouse.

"Nice doin' business with you, Lawler. Let me know when you need a new shipment. Maybe you'd be interested in getting your hands on some weapons. I hear there's a war brewing."

"Yeah, maybe, Kavanagh," I say, brushing off his jibe about weapons. He knows full well I don't deal in guns. That was Theo's business and now Rogers', among other things.

We make it back to my bike before Roxanne gives any sign she's pissed at me, if you don't count the numerous half-moon indents she's left in the side of my hand. Breaking our hand hold to grab the helmets, I turn, offering hers to her, to see she's standing with her hip cocked and her arms folded over her chest.

I find her stance and the scowl she's wearing amusing, but I don't have time to revel in it. I shove the helmet into her chest, and say, "Get on the fucking bike, Roxanne. This is not a place you want to be left alone." She stares at me for what feels like the longest time before she snatches the helmet and puts it on.

I do the same and climb on, offering her my hand as she steps forward to climb on behind me.

"Fuck you," she spits out, shoving my outstretched hand aside.

I pull into the garage, and Roxanne is off the bike before I've even killed the engine. I've just got the stand down and placed my feet on the floor ready to climb off when she shoves me. It's not hard enough to push me off balance, so I jump off the bike and go after her as she stomps toward the house, opening the door and slamming it closed in my face. Getting inside, I see her heading for the stairs and give chase.

"Roxanne," I bellow after her, and she increases her speed up the stairs, taking two at a time. I reach her just as she attempts to shut the door in my face for the second time tonight. I'm getting pretty fucking pissed about that. Jamming my foot in the door, she shoves hard against it, but it's like having a toddler stomping on my foot and does nothing.

"Stop being so damn childish," I taunt, giving a little experimental push on the door. The door swings open in an instant, and had I not been ready for it, I'd be on the floor. I step inside the room as Roxanne steps into me, fronting me up.

"Childish? Fucking childish, Maddox. This is not childish, slamming the door twice earlier was childish. This? This is me preventing a murder. Your fucking murder for putting me in a situation I had no control over, no fucking idea about. And drugs? Jesus fucking Christ, what the hell is wrong with you?" She spins away from me, but in the blink of an eye, her hand connects with my face. I let her have that one, but when she swings again, I snatch her wrist mid-air and drag her forwards. She flails wildly, trying to escape my hold, and when she lands a sneaky punch to my ribcage, I grunt at the impact, almost releasing her.

Any buzz from the line of charlie has well and truly gone now, and I'm more than fucked off with being swung at. Throwing her over my shoulder, she shouts and hollers for me to put her down, so I do.

Dumping her on the bed, the air is knocked out of her for a split second from the impact, just long enough for me to cage her in, pinning her wrists to the bed above her head.

"Stop fucking fighting me and listen."

"Listen? To what exactly, huh? You've given me nothing. A whole lot of fucking trouble and threats but nothing else." She takes a breath, turning her face from mine.

Holding both her hands in one of mine, I bring the other to her face, turning her back to look at me. "You need to trust me." As soon as the words leave my mouth, I know they were the wrong ones.

She lets out a mocking laugh. "Trust you?" Her eyes narrow, and she raises her head from the bed a fraction, her lips almost meeting mine. "I'll never fucking trust you again. You had my trust for four years, Maddox. You and Zak were the only ones I trusted. But you ruined it. Fucking obliterated it. So don't you dare ask me to trust you."

Her words fucking gut me. I know what we did to her, but she doesn't understand. I see the truth in her eyes. She hates us. But I see more there too. Feelings from long ago, and I watch as her chest rises with anger, the pulse at her neck fluttering wildly, and as I adjust my position above her, my groin brushes hers. I know she can feel me, feel how turned on I am, and her eyes spark with arousal.

Her tongue flicks out, wetting her bottom lip, and my eyes

follow it. When my eyes meet hers again, I see the challenge in them, taunting me to make a move. And I do.

Tilting my hips, I watch as her back bows, it's minute but enough to invite me in further. I do it again, and this time her lips part on a silent moan, and I'm gone. Slamming my lips down on hers, I grind my hips again, harder this time. She fights it, but as my tongue delves into her mouth, taking what we both need, I thrust my hips once more, and she relents. My free hand wraps around her throat, and she whimpers as she bucks beneath me, chasing relief from this burning desire running through us both. A desire fuelled by years of pent-up anger and hate.

I don't care that she doesn't trust me. I don't care that she hates me, is pissed at me. All I care about in this moment is stripping her down and fucking her till she understands she's mine.

Breaking the kiss, I tear my jacket and t-shirt off, tossing them aside, then I grip her waist, lifting her and tossing her further up the bed. She flops back down breathlessly, watching me intently and taking in every inch of my body with swollen lips and arousal blown pupils. I sit back on my haunches and strip her jeans from her body. As my eyes land on her black lacy thong, I let out a growl.

Unable to wait another second, I dip down, inhaling her scent and licking a trail up her pussy through her underwear. Needing to taste her, my fingers wrap around the flimsy string of her thong and tear it from her body. I hear a gasp from Roxanne as the material falls away, revealing her glistening cunt to me.

I dive in, literally, feasting on her swollen flesh and spearing her with my tongue before licking all the way up her seam.

"Fuck," she whispers on a pained groan, bucking her hips as I nip at her clit. I grip her hips, keeping her in place as I eat her out. I slide a finger into her dripping wet heat, pumping in and out a couple of times before adding a second, curling them to hit her G-spot.

Roxanne begins to pant as her release nears, and when I feel her tighten around my fingers, I withdraw my fingers and pull my mouth away

"What the...fuck, Maddox," she pants angrily, leaning up on her elbows.

Fuck, she looks beautiful splayed out on the bed, her legs spread and her pussy dripping fucking wet with my saliva and her own juices. I climb from the bed and watch her for a second.

"If you leave me like this, I swear to fucking god—" Her words cut off as I shove my jeans down over my arse, freeing my cock, which is already weeping, and giving it a couple of tugs before I climb between her legs.

I lean forward, rocking my hips and letting my cock glide between the lips of her cunt as I take her mouth, making her taste herself. Taste how fucking sweet she is.

She breaks the kiss on a harsh exhale as I tease her entrance. My mouth trails down her neck, nipping and sucking, no doubt leaving marks on her beautiful skin as the head of my cock breaches the tight walls of her pussy. I hold myself back from entering her any further, torturing us both a little longer. Blocked from tasting anymore of her flesh by the clothes she's still wearing, I push her down onto the bed and take the hem of her t-shirt in my grasp, ripping it open like it was nothing more than paper. Then I roughly shove her bra up, releasing her pert tits with nipples pebbled and begging for my mouth.

"Fuck, Maddox," she whimpers as I lower my head, taking a nipple into my mouth, sucking hard before flicking my tongue over it. I offer the same treatment to the other one, and unable to hold back any longer and feeling her pussy contracting around the head of my cock, trying to draw me in, I slam forward as my teeth bite down on her nipple. She lets out a keening cry at the intrusion and bite of pain as I bury myself to the hilt inside her.

It's fucking heaven as she stretches and wraps around me like a damn glove. After a moment allowing her to adjust to my size, I destroy her. Pounding into her, she meets my every fucking thrust, and when her hand grips my hair, yanking me from her tits roughly, I see the wild look in her eyes as I take her, all of her.

I shift positions, lifting her hips as I sit back on my heels, freeing up my hands and deepening the angle. Keeping one hand at her hip, gripping tightly, I trail the other up her taut stomach, skimming her breast and giving a little flick to her nipple before wrapping my fingers around her delicate neck. Her eyes lock on mine, widening with unadulterated pleasure as I give a little squeeze, temporarily cutting off her oxygen for a second.

"Fuck...yes! I'm...going to...come. Aah...aah," she pants, clamping down on me, and I tighten my hold on her throat again, her legs squeezing around me begin to shake in response as she comes apart. Her eyes roll to the back of her head as wave after wave of pleasure rips through her.

"Look at me, Roxanne. I want you to see who it is that's fucking you, making you scream," I grit out between clenched teeth as my own release crests.

Her eyes snap to mine just as my cock swells, spilling inside her and coating her walls with my seed. My thrusts falter slightly as pleasure short circuits my brain, and I drop my head back on a roar.

As the intense pleasure wanes, I feel Roxanne shift in my still tight grip, and I release her hip, no doubt leaving bruises. That sends a spark of possessiveness through me I didn't think I was capable of.

Looking down at her, I expected to see contentment or at the least a sly smile, but instead I'm met with her face turned away, eyes closed, her mouth turned downward and brows pinched together.

"Hey," I say, shifting and easing out of her. I watch her face the whole time and don't miss the wince as I do. "Shit, did I hurt you, T—"

"Don't say it, Maddox," she warns. "Please, just leave," she says, her tone full of contrition as she climbs from the bed, grabbing her robe and wrapping it tightly around herself.

Anger chases away the pleasure from moments ago, and I rise to my feet, yanking my jeans up as I stride after her. "What the fuck is going on? Did I hurt you?" I grab her arm, pulling her to a stop and spinning her round to face me.

"Hurt me?" she questions, almost like she's not sure what I mean. "Nah, Maddox, you didn't hurt me." I breathe an internal sigh of relief, but it's short lived as she says the next words. "How can you hurt someone you already destroyed?" She can't even look me in the eye, and I shake her, trying to get her to face me. Gripping her chin, I turn her head, but she smacks my hand away, pulling out of my hold on her arm as anger surges in my veins.

She looks dejected as she stands there, arms wrapped around herself as though she's holding herself together.

"Get out."

"No fucking way. It's not how this goes, Roxanne."

"Get out," she says again, firmer this time.

"No," I say, taking a step toward her.

She surges forward and shoves me, much as she did downstairs in the garage, but with more force this time. I wasn't expecting it and am knocked off balance slightly, but she doesn't relent, she keeps coming, shoving me over and over.

"Get the fuck out! Go!" she screams, continuing to push

at me until I find myself in the hall and her door slamming shut on me as she yells, "Leave me the hell alone."

I hear the rustle of fabric on the other side of the door before a small thud, then what sounds like crying. The sound hurts deep in my gut, my heart, and I want to break the door down to get to her, but I know it's probably not a great idea.

"Fuck," I whisper, rubbing a hand across my face. A hand that smells of her, her scent, her arousal, and it makes me hard and my blood boil beneath my skin at the same time.

Needing to get some space, I trudge downstairs and out the front door. I don't know where I'm going, but I need to make someone suffer like I am.

I turn back around and head for the cellar instead.

Chapter Seventeen

Roxy

I feel sick as my legs buckle beneath me, and I slide to the floor, my head giving a soft thud as I drop it back to rest against the door.

Staring up at the ceiling doesn't keep the tears at bay. The ones that have been threatening to spill over since the reality of what just happened hit me like a wrecking ball.

Everyone knows angry sex is the best sex, but angry sex with a guy who stole your first kiss and then promptly abandoned you the same night your world imploded? Yeah, that's the kind of sex that rips you wide open and leaves you bleeding out on the ground.

I know the moment he walks away. I can hear his angry, thunderous steps as he descends the stairs.

My stomach knots impossibly tighter as I allow the sob I've been holding back to finally break free.

I don't know how long I sit there lost in my own head, but a soft vibrating sound stirs me from my place on the floor.

Climbing to my feet, I open the robe and reach into the pocket of the leather jacket I'm still wearing, pulling my phone free, but it rings off just as I get it out.

Not in the mood to talk to anyone, I throw it on the bed and strip out of the robe, dropping it next to my phone. As I pull the jacket from my body, the new leather smell from earlier is mixed with a scent that is all Maddox, and I toss it away quickly.

Looking down at my body, my boobs are still hanging out the bottom of my bra, and the two sides of my now ruined t-shirt flap against my skin. There are red marks, which will be bruises by the morning, on my hips in the perfect shape of Maddox's fingers. Quickly stripping, I pad solemnly across the room to the en-suite, which is a godsend right now, and ignore the dampness between my thighs. As I switch the shower on, I catch my reflection in the mirror and really wish I hadn't.

My eyes are puffy, and streaks of mascara have run down my face, and as I tilt my head, I spot several hickies darkening my neck.

"Fucking hell, Rox!" I admonish myself as I lean forward and inspect my neck a little closer.

There was a time when I would have worn his mark with pride, now I just feel disgusted with myself. How could I have allowed my fucking vagina to rule over my head? If I didn't have cum dripping down my leg and that delicious ache that comes with having been royally and utterly fucked, I'd think I was a guy who's second head ruled the first. What the hell was I thinking?

Turning away from my reflection, I step into the shower, letting the near scolding water cascade over my body. The rain-drop shower head makes the hot water feel like a thousand pin pricks against my skin, and the dull, mildly irritating pain is just what I need to snap me out of my misery and get my head back on straight.

I spend an indeterminable amount of time scrubbing my skin, and by the time I finally switch the shower off and climb out, the water has run cold, and my skin is pink and overly sensitive.

I gently pat my skin dry and towel dry my hair, giving it a quick brush before slowly padding back to the bedroom for the cosy PJ's I bought. The flimsy babydolls I purchased aren't going to cut it tonight, and I feel far from sexy.

Once dressed, I hang the leather jacket in the wardrobe and climb into bed, thankful Maddox's scent isn't on the inside of the covers.

Snuggling down, I return the call I missed. As soon as I hear her voice, I breakdown.

"Oh my fucking god, Roxy, what's going on? You never cry, and if this is something to do with those shithead brothers, I'm going to do some serious arse kicking."

I can't help the laugh that slips free at her threat of violence and rage on my behalf. Swiping the tears from my eyes, I proceed to tell her everything, and when I'm done, the relief is immediate.

"I honestly don't know what to say, girl. This is a crazy mess." I hear her sigh down the phone. "You know that what happened between you and Maddox isn't all bad, right?"

"How's that, Jess? I just screwed a guy who broke my heart, and despite everything he and Zak have done to me then and now, I fucking enjoyed every second. It was the best sex I've ever had. And I've had a lot of sex. What the hell am I supposed to do now? If I stay here, I can't say it won't happen again."

"Well, maybe you can do Zak next time," she jokes, bringing a smile to my face.

"Don't fucking joke." The guy had me rubbing up and down his fucking leg like a cat that's OD'd on catnip. "Arrrgh," I groan. "How the fuck did my life get fucked up so fast?"

"Okay, joking aside, let's forget the hot, angry sex you just had, tell me how this whole thing is going to work with Rogers. Like what's the deal there?"

"That's just it, Jess, I don't fucking know. Maddox told me that the shit at the warehouse tonight is the start of me getting my answers, but answers to what I have no fucking clue?"

"Is it possible that they actually know something about what happened to your mum and sister," she asks hesitantly, knowing it's not a subject I talk about much.

The thought had crossed my mind, but I don't see how they could. They claimed to have information, it's part of why I agreed to help them, but how and what? I need to speak to Mitch about any new leads. I know the body they found recently wasn't Star's, and over the years, there have been a dozen or so possible sightings, which have all amounted to nothing. The night my mum was murdered, Star vanished. It's one of the reasons I was so keen to join CID, especially interested in any human trafficking cases, but there's never been even the smallest hint that's where she ended up.

"I don't think so. I think this is about something else. I just haven't figured out what yet." My mind wanders until Jess' voice draws my attention back to her.

"Roxy, you there?"

"Yeah, sorry. I've got another call, and I need to take it. Can I give you a call back later?"

We say our goodbyes with me promising to call her and after receiving a short lecture on how things happen for a reason.

Even though it's late, I send a message to Mitch asking him to get me another copy of the file on my mum's murder case along with everything he has that we've collected over the years on Star. Thanks to my house burning down, I've lost everything. Years of notes and details, and some of which I'll never get back.

After that, I shoot a quick message to Noah, who is undoubtedly still not talking to me after the last time we spoke, but he needs a head's up on Kavanagh. The guy is bad news. And I'd also be interested in what he can dig up on him.

Jess mentioning my mum and sister has a new sadness wind its way into my tormented mind. Why the hell not? Seems like it's throw all the shit at Roxy just lately. Pride comes before a fall pops into my mind, and I don't particularly like the connotations of that little proverb, especially in the biblical sense. Tempted by the devil, or devils in this case, is right on the fucking money though.

I allow myself some time for a pity party for one and to wallow while I try to fall asleep, but it's impossible. My mind won't shut down and allow me some peace. I check my phone to see it's almost 2am, and I've not heard anyone moving around in the house for the last couple of hours.

Getting up, I pull my robe on and quietly open the bedroom door and tiptoe down the stairs. It's dark, but in the kitchen the blinds are open, and the moonlight lights the room enough for me to find the kettle.

I've barely been in here since I arrived and haven't eaten much in the last couple of days either. My stomach growls in response to my thoughts of food.

I make tea and rummage around in the fridge for something to appease my hunger for now. For two guys, their fridge is surprisingly well stocked, but nothing jumps out at me. I decide to try the cupboards instead and quickly find the cereal cupboard. Who doesn't love cereal as a midnight snack, right?

I'm just putting the first mouthful to my lips when the I hear the front door opening and closing softly behind whoever it is.

From my position perched on the counter with my legs crossed, I can't see into the main hall, but the soft fall of footsteps gets louder as they head this way.

"Shit," I whisper, knowing I don't have time to escape before they reach here. With no other choice, I eat my cereal. The under-cupboard LED lighting flicks on, casting a warm glow around the kitchen, but for me it feels like a damn spotlight.

I watch as Zak wanders into the room, still wearing the same clothes from earlier this evening, although a little more dishevelled now. He looks tired, and his browny-blond hair is messy like he's been running his hand through it, and as if to prove my point, he reaches up and does just that at the same time he turns my way. His hand pauses a fraction of a second halfway through his hair as he spots me, then he continues ruffling his hair further and walking towards the fridge.

He takes out a bottle of beer, opening it and downing half before taking a breath and leaning his shoulder against the fridge.

I feel him watching me, almost scorching my flesh with the intensity. I finish my cereal and place the bowl down on the counter, and when I turn back to look at him, he's now standing right next to me. His hand stretches the small distance, fingertips pushing my chin away from him and tilting my head to the light. I know exactly what he's looking at, and a sliver of shame works its way back into my mind. I push it away, which allows for my snarky, bitchier side to rise to the occasion.

"So, I guess you lost the bet then?" I say, pulling my face from his touch.

"Is that really what you think?" he asks with a contemptuous laugh and steps to stand in front of me. His close proximity makes me edgy, and I can't help the small flinch as he takes my chin again, cupping it and forcing me to look at him. "There was no bet, Rox. There's no competition between Mad and I when it comes to you. And in case you missed it back then, which I know you didn't, you've only ever been ours. You might not believe it or feel it fully right now, but here with us is exactly where you were always meant to be." He leans down, gripping my chin harder, and lays a delicate kiss on my lips.

His lips are soft as they meet mine, and I can taste the beer he just drank, dark and delicious and tempting in all the wrong ways. I know it's wrong. I just spent the last few hours berating myself and full of shame at my inability to keep these two out of my mind and body, but it seems to all vanish the instant one of them touches me, gets too close, or hell, even talks to me.

Zak deepens the kiss, brushing his tongue across the seam of my bottom lip, and I open, permitting him entry and parting as easily as a whore's legs.

The thought is like a cold bucket of ice as Kavanagh's words come back to me, and I pull back quickly, banging my head on the cupboard behind me.

"Ow, fuck!" I rub at the sore spot, inching as far back from Zak as possible. Maybe a bang to the head is what I need to knock some fucking sense back into me. Hell knows I need it.

"Jeez, Rox, you okay?" He raises his hands, reaching to pull my head and get a better look, but I dodge them and push him away as I drop down to the floor.

"I'm fine, just leave it, Zak. I'm going to head back to bed. Night," I tell him, hurrying from the kitchen.

"Sweet dreams, Rox," he calls after me, followed by a dark chuckle that follows me all the way to my room, and it's only when I've closed the door that it drifts away.

I flop down onto the bed face first, thumping my fist into the mattress a dozen or more times out of frustration at...well, everything.

I roll over and make a new plan, and top of the list is to move out of this house. There's no way I can stay here in a house full of temptation; a temptation that slides through my hate and anger like a damn knife through butter.

I need to show my face at the station tomorrow, despite knowing how that's going to play out. Even when I'm cleared and the corruption charges are dropped, my reputation will be dog shit. More so when my connection to Maddox and Zak emerges, which it will and soon after last night.

There's no way Kavanagh won't be talking it up that the great Roxanne Whitmore was at an exchange with one of the Lawlers.

I'm waiting for the backlash to come. I've already been racked over the coals in the press, and with the incident at the supermarket, it won't be long before the anti-police brigade come out in full force.

Chapter Eighteen

Zak

Rox hurries from the kitchen, and I can't help tease her a little more. "Sweet dreams, Rox," I call, letting out a dark chuckle. I finish off my beer and grab another from the fridge. As I close the door, Maddox is standing there with a deep scowl on his face.

"Have a good time?" I ask, raising my brows before taking a large mouthful of my new beer. He scoffs as I move aside and lean against the counter where Rox was previously sitting, her scent still lingering.

"What did you find out about the girl?" Maddox asks, taking out a beer for himself and ignoring my taunting about what happened with him and Rox. I don't need him to draw me a fucking picture. Rox's swollen eyes, jittery temperament and a neck that looks like the vampire Lestat enjoyed a good meal are evidence enough.

"Fuck all. I sat outside her house, a nice house for someone of her age by the way, all night. Nobody entered, and she only left once to collect food. Whoever she is, last night told me nothing." I swig my beer before asking, "And our guest, he give you anything new?"

"Nothing that makes me think he's worth keeping alive." There's a hint of sadness about that. Axel has been with us since we split from Theo and has always been loyal and dependable before now.

"What do you want to do? Something doesn't feel right about this whole situation, Mad."

"I know, but what the fuck do you want me to do, Zak? We can't be seen to have any weakness, not now. And he's not giving me shit to make me think twice about finishing him. If he was anyone else or this was any other time, he'd already be dead."

"You could let Rox have a shot at him."

Maddox chokes on his beer at my suggestion, and when he's recovered enough to speak, he says, "What the fuck, Zak?"

"She saw me with him earlier." His eyes narrow. "She was pissed, sure, but have you forgotten who she is? She's built her whole reputation on locking up dozens of hardened criminals. Besides, she's no wall flower, Mad. It's worth a shot. I take it you left him breathing?"

"For now, yes." He downs his beer, and a frown creases his brow.

"Want to talk about it?" I ask, not really expecting him to, so when he answers, I'm surprised.

"I took her to the meet with Kavanagh. She wasn't happy with me snorting a line of the goods, and well, need I say more."

"I bet that went over well. I'm surprised you're still standing. How did Kavanagh take her being there?"

"Surprisingly well. Maybe a little too well as he didn't question her presence at all." He frowns, and I know that's bothering him. The fact Kavanagh didn't question her motives or wasn't concerned she may have been there in a more formal capacity is a little worrying. "Anyway, the deals done, and the new shipment is stashed at the warehouse.

There are only four people that know where that shipment is, so if this one goes walkabout, then I know where to point my finger."

"How long you going to keep it there?"

"At least a week. That gives whoever the fuck is messing with our shipments more than enough time. I had Bowser bring me back a few kilos to keep the buyers happy for now."

"Good. Let's hope we can catch another rat bastard, and this one is all mine."

"What's the matter, brother, feeling a little twitchy?" He chuckles, taking our empties and dumping then in the bin.

"Axel was just the appetiser, whetting my appetite, and now I'm fucking starved." I place Roxy's bowl in the sink and move to head upstairs when Maddox stops me.

"Zak, you really think I should let Roxy have at him?"

"Why the hell not. Look, the worst she can do is say no, and after that, nothing lost nothing gained." I give a shrug, then say, "I'm done, man. Catch you in the morning."

He nods. "Night."

I pause outside Roxy's door and contemplate whether to check on her, but I decide against it. Sounds like she's had more than enough fun tonight. Besides, I need her at least a little amenable if I'm going to convince her to question Axel.

Despite not going to bed till almost 3am, I'm up just after seven. What few hours I did manage were filled with my demons scratching at my mind.

When I reach the kitchen, I find Maria there preparing breakfast, and my mouth waters and my stomach grumbles at the delicious scent of bacon cooking.

She's been away for a couple of days, visiting a friend

who's just come out of hospital, and no doubt hasn't a clue about our new guest.

She places a plate down on the breakfast bar as I grab myself a glass of orange juice from the fridge.

"Will Miss Whitmore be joining you this morning," she questions with a raised brow, and I almost choke on my juice.

"Damn, Maria, are you trying to kill me?" She passes me a cloth to wipe up the mess I made. "How the hell do you do that? You've barely been back five minutes."

She chuckles as she takes the cloth back and replaces my empty glass with a cup of tea. "Don't be so melodramatic, Zak."

Maddox enters just as I'm laying my cutlery on my plate.

"Morning," he grumbles, taking the tea Maria offers him and joins me at the breakfast bar. I don't get to ask him anything else as his phone rings. Pulling it from his pocket, he frowns at whoever is calling him at this time in the morning.

I listen as he answers, his voice gruff and pissed off already. I can't hear the voice on the other end, but I sure as shit hear Maddox when he lets out a deafening reply.

"Fucking hell! How in God's fucking name is this possible, huh?" I faintly hear the person on the other end as they talk. "No, don't move anything. I'll be there as soon as." He ends the call, dropping his phone to the counter with a clunk as the armoured case meets the marble.

I don't really need him to tell me what's happened because his reaction, the tic in his jaw and the metaphorical steam billowing from his ears is enough.

"They took it, right?"

"Of course, they fucking did, Zak. Every damn time for the last three shipments. It wasn't even there twelve hours, for fuck's sake. He's fucking toying with us. Axel knows more than he's telling us. He's going to tell me today before I rip his tongue from his fucking head and deliver it in person to his mother."

"Well, isn't this a pleasant conversation to have over breakfast. I'm so glad I came down here for it," says a voice behind us. All eyes turn to Roxy who is standing just inside the door to the kitchen wearing the same pyjamas and robe as last night. Only this time she has the collar of the robe turned up in an attempt, I'm sure, to cover up the bite marks and hickies I saw last night. She steps into the room, eyes landing on Maria who smiles knowingly at her.

"Ah, here she is. Please, come and sit. Would you like some tea or coffee, Miss Whitmore?" Maria asks, gesturing to an empty seat at the breakfast bar.

"She'll have tea, white no sugar," Maddox says, and Rox's eyes immediately snap to his.

"*She* can speak for herself." Turning to Maria, she says, "A tea would be great, thanks." Ignoring the empty seat at the breakfast bar, Rox stalks past both of us and drops down into a chair at the dining table.

I look at Maddox, who's eyes have tracked every movement she's made since she so eloquently announced her presence.

"I take it Axel is your other prisoner?" she probes, bringing one foot up to rest on the chair and dropping her chin to it.

"You're not a fucking prisoner, Roxanne," Maddox bites back, and I'm not in the least bit ashamed to admit their snarkiness turns me on.

"My cage is certainly better than his, but let's call a spade a spade, shall we." Without giving Maddox a chance to volley back at her, she continues, "Why's he here?" She thanks Maria as she places her cup of tea in front of her and waits for one of us to answer. Her eyes flick between us. "Well, don't all answer at once," she says with a roll of her eyes, bringing the cup to her lips and blowing gently before taking a sip.

Climbing from my stool, I walk over and take the seat opposite her. "Let's just say he has information we want, but I think he's holding back because he's protecting someone." I pull out my phone and load up the details I have for Eva Trent.

"Isn't he one of your guys?" she asks, frowning.

I nod, turning the phone and handing it to her. "Do you know her?"

I watch as she scans the details I have on Eva, then they widen before immediately snapping up to mine.

"You don't know who she is, do you?"

Maddox and I share a look before I look back to her. "No, but you obviously do. So, who is she?"

She passes me my phone back and takes several sips of her tea before answering, and I can almost see the cogs turning in her head.

"What do you want with her?"

"Fuck that. This is not how it works, Roxanne," Maddox states.

Rox shrugs. "From where I'm sitting, this is exactly how it works. You want my help, then you tell me why you're interested in her. Simple."

"You can't help yourself can you," I say with a half-smile and shaking my head. She seems different this morning. Last night she seemed dejected, sad and her walls were down. Now though, the walls are back up, and she's ready to fight.

I explain to her that I saw Eva coming out of Axel's place, but not the two of them together. I also give enough detail about why Axel is being held downstairs but leave out any mention of names for now. Maddox fires daggers engulfed in flames at me from the breakfast bar the whole time.

"So, you think that Axel is in a relationship with Eva, or at the very least working with her?" I nod, and she frowns deeply. "If this is who he's protecting then what?"

"That depends on who she is, Roxanne."

"Okay, I'll tell you who she is, but you need to promise no harm will come to her, and you need to tell me what the fuck was going on in Oxford Street yesterday."

Maddox steps into her space, crouching to eye level with her. "I'm making no such promise, and as for what happened in Oxford Street, you best get used to it. Welcome back to the underworld, Roxanne."

Rox leans forward, so she's an inch away from his face. "And you best start giving me some fucking answers, Maddox, or this whole thing is off. My career is already over, so whatever you think you have on me is kind of useless now. I want answers about my mum and sister, and that's all I'm here for."

I watch their standoff, eyes focused solely on one another and setting the temperature in the room alight with sexual tension. From the corner of my eye, I even see Maria swallow thickly before leaving the room looking flushed and though she witnessed them fucking on the table not just having a conversation.

It's getting fucking uncomfortable in my boxers watching, and I need to do something before I whip my dick out right here in the middle of the kitchen and jack off.

"Rox, you and I can talk about the shit in Oxford Street, but Maddox has some other *business* he needs to attend to, so how about you just tell us who she is."

At first, I don't think either of them have heard me, but Rox eventually turns her head my way.

"You're not going to like this, but you can't hurt her. She's not involved and doesn't know anything."

Maddox growls his disapproval but nods.

Taking a deep breath, Rox says, "Her real name is Eva Laskin. She's Laskin's daughter."

The air in the room turns frigid and time stands still for a split second as her words permeate the initial shock and fully sink in.

"Oh fuck!" Is all I manage as I look to Maddox. His face is blank of any emotion, but beneath the surface, I know he's seething. In the second I turn from Maddox and look to Rox, scanning her face for any clue she's lying, Maddox is at the door to the cellar. It crashes against the wall as he throws it open, and I'm out of my seat in the blink of an eye. There's no way I can let him near Axel now. He has somewhere else to be, and with the mood he's in, Axel will be dead before his brain even warns him of the danger.

I reach him just as his foot lands on the first step, clapping a hand around his arm. "You don't want to do this now. You have more important things to focus on. Rox and I will talk to him. Get out of here. Sort out the shit with the shipment," I whisper the last part conscious that Rox is watching us and only a foot away from me having leapt up when I did.

His head turns a fraction, pupils dilated with fury, and I give him a second to make the right decision. A breath rushes from him, and he shrugs my hand away as he turns and steps from the stairwell.

"Hey, someone going to tell me what the fuck is going on?" Roxy says, catching Maddox's arm as he goes to pass her.

His eyes remain on hers as he speaks to me. "Zak, give her what she needs to get answers from Axel. When I get back, we'll fucking talk." He peels her fingers from his arm and yanks her to him, chest to chest. I hear her breath catch as he lowers his face to hers. "Stay in the fucking house, Roxanne." He releases her and walks away before she can reply.

"Arsehole!" Rox calls out, but it's pointless as the front door slams shut and not a minute later an engine revs before tyres squeal away down the drive. Rox walks back to the table and sits down, all the while muttering furiously.

I close the cellar door and join her. "How do you know about Eva?"

"Doesn't matter how I know, the point is that Laskin doesn't, and it needs to stay that way."

"You're telling me that Laskin has a daughter he knows nothing about. How the fuck is that possible, Rox? A man like Laskin would never let something like that go unnoticed."

"Well, it's true. And if you go digging around, all you're going to do is put her life in danger." She twiddles with the handle of her cup contemplatively. "And besides, you and I both know it's entirely possible for a child to fly under the radar, and you also know the fall out when said child comes to light."

I know she's talking about herself and the situation with her biological father. Lord Chief Justice James Whitmore is nothing more than a sperm donor when it comes to Rox. She's never received a fraction of the love and care a father is meant to willingly give to his child. The only thing he's ever done for her is ruin what should have been a beautiful childhood.

Maddox and I both know how Rox's mum, Tracey, ended up a worn-out junkie whore, and it wasn't by choice. After Tracey's affair with James, she fell pregnant, and despite buying her off with abortion and silence money, she managed to keep Rox hidden for years.

But the truth always comes out, and once he discovered Rox's existence, he systematically destroyed everything Tracey had built.

Not wanting to dredge up the past, one I know hurts, and with the inevitability the conversation will turn toward questions about why she's here, which I can't give her answers to right now, I fill her in on Axel.

She listens raptly as I explain how Axel came to be where he is and what both Maddox and I have managed to ascertain from him. She interrupts a couple of times to ask questions or verify details. I don't mention Bonner or the shipments. I'm not stupid and neither is Rox. She knows I'm not giving her the whole picture, but she doesn't call me out on it for now.

"I want to talk to him alone," she states when I've finished.

"Hell fucking no, Rox. That is never happening."

"If you want my help, then, yeah, it fucking is happening! Come on, Zak, do you honestly believe he'll give you anything with you standing guard over him?" She raises her brows at me in question, and I know she's probably right. "You can wait right outside but out of sight."

I can see the anticipation and eagerness for my agreement written all over her face. Maddox will string me up and gut me like a damn pig if he finds out.

"Fine. But I'll be outside the door, and if he so much as breathes on you the wrong way, then it's done. And don't tell—"

"Maddox. Yeah, I got it. Wouldn't want him to possibly think I can look after myself after all this time." She rolls her eyes but smiles too.

Chapter Nineteen

Roxy

I ask Zak for a first aid kit, and while he gets it, I fill a glass with water and make a sandwich. When he returns with it, he looks at me quizzically.

"For Axel," I state like it should be obvious. "I know this might be a concept you aren't familiar with but being nice works sometimes." I don't voice the rest of that thought. A good cop, bad cop joke probably won't go over too well just now.

Once I have everything, Zak opens the door to the cellar, letting me go first. He knows I've been down here when he was questioning Axel, if you can call it that, the other day.

I prepare myself for the sight and smell I know I'm going to be met with as Zak opens the door to the first room.

A single bulb hanging from the ceiling fills the space and highlights the dank interior. It's basically a concrete cell with nothing but a bucket to piss in. Axel is laying on his back either asleep or unconscious in the middle of the room. I can see from here that there are several more bruises to his body and injuries to his face since Zak was here last, which makes me think Maddox has been here at some point.

Despite feeling aroused by watching Zak the other day, I struggle to comprehend what I'm now faced with. It makes me sick to think I could be turned on watching a man torturing another man. I don't honestly know what to make of the whole thing.

I step inside, turning to ensure Zak is sticking to his side of the deal and remaining outside. Our eyes meet, and for the first time since they crashed back into my life, I see a flicker of uncertainty. He drops my gaze and pulls the door to a fraction.

A groan draws my attention back to the man on the floor. A man who is by no means small and no doubt is handsome when half his face isn't covered with cuts, bruises and dried blood.

I step forward and kneel beside him, setting the first aid kit, sandwich and water on the floor. He's not wearing any clothing except his underwear. Scanning my eyes over him, I see the word rat crudely sliced into his skin, and I already know whose handy work that is.

"Fuck," I murmur into the cold, empty room. Another groan comes from Axel, and this time his head turns my way. He opens his eyes, one still badly swollen, and he starts to panic when he sees me. "Hey, it's okay, Axel. I'm not here to hurt you." He stops trying to move, which I realise is painfully hard for him given the abuse that has been inflicted upon him.

"I know who you are," he hisses. "What do you want?"

I spot a chair over the other side of the room and rising to my feet, I collect it. "I just want to talk, Axel. Can you get up?" He pushes himself up, a grimace on his face the whole time and holding his breath, which comes out in a rush as he comes to rest sitting upright. After a few deep breaths, he attempts to climb to his feet, falling slightly with a cry of pain as he bends, no doubt from a few broken ribs. I do my best to help him, despite his protests, and finally get him seated in the chair.

While he catches his breath again, I kneel on the floor and

open the first aid kit. Once his breathing has settled, I hand him the glass of water. His hand shakes as he takes it from me, spilling some over the side. I watch as a big fat drop splats to his knee, dispersing some of the grime that covers his skin.

He gulps it down and passes me the empty glass. I feel his eyes on me as I put it down and then root around inside the first aid box for what I need.

"I can't tell you anything, so if that's what this little show of hospitality is for, then you're wasting your time."

"It's nice to see you still have your balls, or is that because I'm a woman and you're either not scared or trying to save face?" He doesn't answer, just stares mutely at me with what I can only imagine are hard eyes. "Anyway, I'm here for answers, of course, but don't be fooled by my nice gesture, Axel. There is more than one way to skin a cat. And despite what you just said, I know you have the answers, so let's not waste both our time," I say, easily slipping into my cop persona.

"You can do whatever the fuck you want to me, but I'll never tell you anything."

"Okay, well, I beg to differ. And the reason for that is because I know about Eva." The flicker of his eyes and infinitesimal inhale of breath are the only signs that I'm right, so I push a little more. "The way I see it, if you don't want any harm to come to Eva, then I guess you best start talking. I'm not so sure Eva can hold up against the Lawlers as well as you seem to be."

"You leave her the fuck alone." And there it is. The tiniest nugget of information that comes from the biggest motivator of all, love. "She's nothing to do with this."

"Ahh, come on, you don't honestly believe that do you? And here's another reason why you're going be singing out your confession in a minute, but just as a precursor before I get to that, Zak is right outside the door and that means you're going to take this like the honourable man you so obviously are or risk putting Eva in the firing line more than she already is. Understand?" He nods, and I can see he knows what's coming before I've even said it. "I not only know about Eva, but I also know, as do Maddox and Zak, who her father is, her real father. So, let's try this again, tell me what you know?"

Zak comes into the room as a dejected Axel spills his guts while I clean him up. When Zak finally has all the answers he's going to get, I hand Axel the sandwich I made him, and we leave, ignoring his protests and demands to know what's going to happen to him now.

Back in the kitchen, I dump the first aid kit on the counter and spin to face Zak.

He's running his hand through his hair, and I feel as though he's mentally pacing up and down as he thinks about the information Axel shared.

"What are you thinking?" I ask, knowing that there are only two real options of what to do with him now. One of which I'm not even sure I can pull off, but I'll damn well try, if not for Axel, then at least for Eva and their unborn child.

"I'm thinking about all the ways I can cut that fucker up."

I know he's not lying. I can see it clear as day on his face. "But?" I question. The fact he hasn't already done so means there's a definite but.

"But I don't fucking know, Rox."

"I have a suggestion. It's not going to be a popular one with you and definitely not with Maddox, but it's an option."

"Let me guess, you want to put them in police protection or some similar shit, right?" he says disdainfully.

"Maybe don't let the distaste in your words drip so colourfully next time, but, yeah, it's a possibility."

He steps toward me as I lean against the counter. "Maddox will never go for it. And I can't say I'm that keen either."

"And why's that, Zak?" I ask, folding my arms across my body. I'm not sure if it's to protect myself from his proximity and alluring eyes, scent, body, hell, the whole package, or if it's purely to demonstrate my dislike of him questioning a system that's been my life.

He takes another step forward, invading my personal space, which seems to be something him and Maddox enjoy a little too much. "Because it's bullshit. The police can't protect people from the likes of Laskin and Bonner and Rogers. Your precious police force is as corrupt as the rest of the governing institutions in this world, Rox."

"Does that little list include you and Maddox too, Zak? Are there people that need protection from you? Do you have a cop in your pocket who is willing to sacrifice his oath and integrity to save his own skin and line his pockets with blood money?" I can't help the edge of anger that comes out in my words.

"Nobody can protect you from us, Rox, not even yourself. If we have you in our sights, there isn't a force on this earth that can keep you safe." He steps right into me, so we are almost touching but not quite.

I don't think he's talking about other people anymore. I get the feeling his words are solely for my benefit, and it sends a tendril of fear and pleasure surging through me.

I promised I wouldn't allow them to pull me in, that I would keep my distance and harden myself to this magic and energetic pull they seem to have over me, but it's not working very fucking well because I just can't seem to stop it.

My mouth opens and words pour from it before my brain can catch up. "Why are you doing this, Zak? What did I do to you and Maddox that was so bad you'd tear up my life like this, huh?" There's a flicker of remorse that's gone as quick as it appeared. Even after all these years he still struggles to conceal his feelings fully.

"There are a lot of things you've done, Rox, and things you don't know, but none—" His phone rings, cutting him off. I silently pray that he'll ignore it and finish what he was telling me, but when he pulls it free and sees who's calling, he steps away without a second thought.

I watch as he walks off down the hall, passing Maria as she enters the kitchen.

"Would you like tea, Miss Whitmore?" she asks as she fills the kettle.

"Er...it's Roxy, and tea would be great, thanks." She nods, pulling down two cups from the cupboard. I watch absent-mindedly as she drops a teabag in each cup and adds milk just as the kettle boils.

I don't really understand how she can act so damn normal when just a few hours ago Maddox was in here screaming about a shipment of charlie and threatening to rip someone's tongue out. They have cells in their cellar, and I'm certain the irony hasn't gone unnoticed, where they are holding a guy, a so-called friend, who has taken one hell of a beating and bears the word rat on his skin. How is this considered normal?

A soft chink sounds behind me, and I turn to see Maria has placed my tea on the counter.

"Thank you," I say, drawing my tea closer toward me so that I can wrap my hands around it. They are suddenly cold. It's a perfect parallel to the cold feeling I've had in the pit of my stomach for the last two and bit weeks.

"You'll get used to it," Maria states as she brings her own tea over and takes a seat on a stool at the breakfast bar the other side to me. "I certainly never expected my life to be filled with death and destruction when I married my husband all those years ago. It's funny what you get used to when you have no choice, and when you love someone, of course. That changes everything."

"I'm sorry, but I don't understand how you ever get used to this."

"No need to be sorry, dear, it is what it is. What you need

to remember is that many of us never asked for this life, never wanted or even imagined it. That's the funny thing about life though, isn't it? Things rarely turn out how you want them to."

"It doesn't bother you? Because it sure as hell bothers me. My whole life has been about protecting those who find themselves in situations just like this, in this world, and whilst I'm not naive, I..."

"Have you ever considered that you're protecting the wrong people, Roxy?" I go to interrupt, not in the slightest bit impressed with her question. "I know that's a difficult thing to consider, but those men, Maddox and Zak, they have had very little choice in the things they have done, have endured, in the time you've been gone. I know who you are, Roxy, and I know you're not so naive as to think so black and white. Remember where you came from before you became who you are." With that, she picks up her tea and leaves the kitchen, giving me no chance to respond.

I'm a little unsure how to take being schooled by a woman old enough to be my mother. I'd be lying if I said that's what irritates me the most about that whole conversation. It's not. The fact her words are now flying around inside my mind like some uncaged bird pecking away at the worms of truth buried beneath years of rhetoric and conditioning makes me uneasy.

I don't like that she read me so well, questioned my morals and integrity, but what I hate more is the idea that everything she said has even a grain of truth.

I finish my tea and think about what she meant when she said Maddox and Zak had no choice. Then I think about what it means to have no choice. Is there always a choice? At what point do your choices become diminished by external factors or become no choice at all?

I had a choice when my mum became incapable of looking after me and Star. I had a choice when she died, when Star disappeared, but they aren't a choice when the only other option is to starve, to become another statistic in the care system, to forget, to give up on the only person left in your family that means anything to you.

They're not choices at all. They are the difference between life and death, good and bad. They are the decisions that determine who you are as a person.

So, the question is, what were Maddox and Zak's choices when they cut me off, when they decided that a life of crime and murder was more appealing than the possibility of having me in their life and possibly making something better for us all?

I shake the thoughts from my mind because there is no good sitting here asking about what ifs and wondering about answers to questions only Maddox and Zak themselves can give me.

I rinse my cup and place it in the dishwasher, and when there's still no sign of Zak returning, I dash upstairs to grab my phone and car keys.

I know Maddox told me I wasn't to leave the house, but I think it's already been established that I'm not good at following orders from anyone, particularly that man.

I need to go to the station anyway, and I now need to talk to Noah about how to keep Axel and Eva safe.

I slip out of the house, but when I reach the gate, I realise I don't have a fob to open it.

"Shit!" I search the car, hoping that Zak dropped his but no luck. I'm just about to give up when the gates begin opening. Looking up as the creaking metal grinds against one another, I don't see anyone there and no explanation for why the gates are opening. Not one to look a gift horse in the mouth, I drive out.

The station is quiet when I arrive, something I'm thankful for. I can take a lot and have thick skin but knowing how some of my fellow officers will feel about me now is something I'm really not in the mood for.

I head straight for the DCI's office, passing a couple of constables who watch me with hawk eye precision.

There's a gruff command of 'come in' when I knock on the door. I push inside and halt when I see who is already there.

Chapter Twenty

Maddox

I skid to a halt, kicking up gravel, outside the warehouse, which on the outside appears like any other. However, when I step inside, it's a different matter altogether.

"Madd—"

I hold up my hand to Bowser, stopping him from spouting whatever shit was about to spill from his mouth. My eyes scan the warehouse, now empty bar one crate that sits innocuously in the middle of the room. The lid is sitting askew, and the once light wood is now stained a bright red. I step closer, making sure to avoid the growing puddle of blood seeping through the bottom of the crate.

"What's in there?"

"No idea, Maddox. You told me not to touch anything."

I step forward, and using the edge of my t-shirt, I flip the lid off. It lands with a loud clatter on the concrete.

Blank, dead eyes stare up at me from a familiar face inside the crate.

"Fucking hell!" As I look closer, I see an arm and fingers poking out at an impossible angle for a limb still attached to a body. Raw, bloody skin and muscle are visible where his head has been severed from his body. I feel Bowser leaning forward beside me as he looks at the head of Sammy nestled in the crate. A crate full of body parts left here as a message, a warning.

Sammy Evans and his brother, Tommy, have been runners for the past two years. I brought them in after Axel vouched for them. Looks like that was a huge fucking mistake on my part.

Zak suspects that Tommy tipped Rogers off about a meet we'd set up with a new supplier. It's the reason we ended up using Kavanagh, which was something we'd never intended. Getting in bed with the Irish is never a good thing, but between Rogers and Bonner, we'd been left with no other choice. Zak and I suspect that pushing us in that direction is part of Rogers' plan. Following the murder of Theo, Rogers' father, it didn't take long before the whispers of us ordering the hit on Theo began. The fact that the underworld knew of our fallout with Theo prior to his death meant that it wasn't hard for Rogers to fuel the rumours and convince others we were to blame.

Bowser leans forward to look inside. "That's gotta have been painful," he jests.

"No fucking kidding, B. Now, get a clean-up crew here. And I want the name of the person you leased this building from by the time I get home." I step back and inhale deeply, expelling the putrid, rotten flesh smell already beginning to pollute the air. "Where's Rocky? You seen or heard from him since last night?"

"Yeah, called and checked in with him this morning. He's fine based on the soft slurping sounds I could hear in the background," Bowser says with a chuckle and adding, "Lucky bastard."

We walk towards the exit as Bowser puts in a call for a clean-up team.

"You reckon Tommy knows his brother's been chopped up into tiny little pieces?"

I think on it for a second. Based on what Zak told me about Tommy aligning with Bonner, I doubt he knows his brother has been used as bait, nothing more than fodder to lure me into some convoluted little game.

"No, I doubt it, but let's keep that nugget of information between us for now. You never know when it will come in handy." We reach the door, and I remind B to get me the info on who owns this warehouse.

After our last place was hit, three times, we decided to move the shipment to an unknown location, one that has no association to us at all.

Several things about that are still fucking with my head. The rent of the warehouse was made in a false name, and the only people to know of its whereabouts or our connection to it were myself, Zak, Bowser and Rocky. Not even Axel knew about it, not that it matters because the traitorous cunt has been locked up in our cellar for days bleeding his betrayal all over the floor.

As I jump back in my car and head home, my mind turns to Roxanne's revelation about who Eva Trent really is.

Laskin has a daughter.

One he knows fuck all about.

The possibilities of what I can do with that information has a spike of excitement trickling through my veins. But it's halted a second later when I remember Roxanne stating she's not to be harmed, and I'm suddenly wondering what's so damn special about Eva that Roxanne would want to protect her.

I put my foot down now eager to get home and find out

what Zak and Roxanne have managed to get from Axel if anything.

Pulling down the road to our house, I push the fob for the gates as I get closer. When I arrive, the gates have just clanged fully open, and I drive right in, pushing the fob to close the gates as I head for the garage.

Inside the house, I hear Zak talking in the office and head to the kitchen, grabbing a beer from the fridge. My phone pings with a message just as Zak walks in. I quickly open it and see it's from Bowser with the name and address of the owner of the warehouse as requested.

"What happened at the warehouse?"

"Everything is gone. Not a surprise. They did leave us a nice little gift though."

Zak grabs another beer from the fridge, knocking the cap off on the counter and passing it to me and taking the closed one I'm still holding.

"I'll regret asking, but what was the gift." He knocks the cap off his beer and takes a mouthful.

"Sammy Evans." I pause for a couple of seconds before continuing, "Dismembered and packaged up in a crate."

"Nice." There's a tiny spark of reverence in his eyes, but Zak doesn't say anymore.

My brother's mind is not his own when there's a blade and a blank canvas for the taking. Despite the circumstances surrounding our allegiance to Theo Rogers, he was good to us in some ways. Unfortunately, that goodness came at a cost. A very high cost. He was a master at getting inside your mind and doing whatever it took to achieve his goals.

When Zak and I signed our lives away in exchange for another's, he had all the leverage he needed to ensure we did anything he asked of us. The men we are today are a far cry from the two teen boys he enlisted into his family.

"Bowser is with the clean-up crew now. Thank fuck we kept some of it back or we'd have Marchant up our arse. Not that I really give a fuck. I'd like to shoot the cocky little shit, but we need him on side for now. How'd you go with Axel?" His face morphs into one of anger and bitterness.

"Well, he's still alive. He spilled his guts, and it ain't good, Mad. It was Axel that told Rogers where the shipments were going, and he also told him about our deal with Marchant." He pauses, and I know I'm not going to like what's coming next. "He told him we were bringing Roxy back into the fold."

I launch the bottle across the room and beer sprays from the top before it hits the wall, exploding into a shower of glass.

"Son of a fucking bitch!" Red descends over me like a blanket of fog. My mind fills with images of how I'm going to cut that fucker open and make him pay in blood for his betrayal. Before I even know what I'm doing, I have Zak pinned to the wall, my face an inch from his. "Why the fuck is he still breathing, Zak? And you better have a fucking good answer because I'm ready to go to town on your arse for allowing him to take another breath."

"Get your fucking hands off me," he roars, breaking my grip on his t-shirt and shoving me away. "He's still fucking breathing because Roxy would murder the both of us if we lay another finger on him."

I let out an amused scoff. "Fuck that shit!" I barge Zak out of the way as I head for the stairs. "Roxy. Get your arse down here now," I yell as I reach the bottom step. "Roxy!" When she doesn't answer, I bolt up the stairs two at a time and throw her door open.

My mouth opens to unleash on her, but I'm stopped short when I realise the room is empty. My eyes do a quick scan and see her stuff is still here and all still in the bags they were bought in. The fact she hasn't unpacked sends another wave of anger through me.

Zak steps up behind me just as my eyes drift to the window. Her room is at the front of the house and looks out over the driveway. It's only now looking down that I notice something is missing.

"Where's Roxy's car?"

Footsteps sound behind me as Zak strides across the room, joining me at the window.

"Shit!" Zak exclaims, and we both rush from the room. As we hit the landing, Maria comes strolling towards us. "Maria, have you seen Roxy?"

"She went out about thirty minutes ago. What's the problem?" she asks innocently, and I know Maria, she's not fucking innocent at all. "I believe you told her she wasn't a prisoner, or something to that effect."

"I also told her not to fucking leave the house!"

"Yes, well, we all know that was never going to happen. That woman can't be told what do, Maddox. Come on, you know this. Besides, I imagine she's gone to find some answers for herself and fix your problem in the cellar."

"What the fuck are you talking about? And don't talk riddles to me, Maria, I'm not in the mood." I can see Zak in the corner of my eye on his phone. No doubt ringing Roxy, but from the look on his face, he's not having any luck.

"Maddox, you're a smart, yet calculating, man, so surely you didn't fail to consider what impact pulling Roxy from everything she's known for the last ten years would have on her. A life I'm very aware you had a hand in. If you want any chance of getting her to cooperate instead of fighting you, then you're going to have to give her a reason. A damn good one.

"As for your little problem in the cellar, well, you need him. And I know that goes against everything you believe, everything you've had drilled into you. And that's my point,

Maddox." And with that she moves passed me and into her room at the end of the hall.

I round on Zak, who is still attempting to get hold of Roxanne. "I want to know everything, then if she's not back, you'll go and look for her while I head to The Scarlett Door for the meet with Marchant."

I take a couple of semi-calming breaths, which don't touch the sides of my anger. We always knew that bringing Roxanne back would be a problem, and Maria was right, I'd not really considered just how difficult it would be to make her see things differently.

Now, my eyes are wide fucking open.

Changing beliefs that have been ingrained, indoctrinated for years is going to take more than a simple click of my fingers. This is not a case of just ordering her to forget everything she's upheld and lived for, and that is a tough pill to swallow for a guy like me.

Yes, I've changed too, but mine has been an evolution of who I already was, who I was becoming even before Zak and I made the deal with Theo.

After Roxanne's mum was murdered and her sister disappeared, we cut her off, and it was the single hardest thing I've ever had to do. I've killed men with my bare hands. I've blown their brains out while their wife or girlfriend stood beside them. I've sold my soul to the devil a hundred times over and committed it to Hell once my life is done, and I'd do it all again if I had to.

Roxanne has no idea of the danger she's in, no reason to listen when I tell her to stay indoors, no reason to trust me. And that's on me and Zak. Those are the consequences of a decision we made ten years ago.

When Zak begins telling me what happened with Roxanne and Axel in the cellar, I wished I'd been here to see her in her element, in her safe place.

Her methods might differ greatly from ours, but the results are the same. Sometimes.

Only there's no room in this world for the softly, softly approach. There's no room for 'let's wait and see what they do next'. In this world a split second of hesitation will cost you everything.

"Axel has no idea how Rogers found out about Eva. All he knows is that Rogers is threatening to tell Laskin about her. Possibly use her as bait or some shit. Who the hell knows what lengths the wanker will go to get what he wants."

"I'm guessing that's rhetorical because we both know exactly how far Rogers is willing to go. What I really want to know is how Roxanne knew who she was, and why she's so keen to protect her." I check my watch, conscious that I need to be at The Scarlett Door in less than an hour, and there's still no sign of Roxanne. I catch Zak's eye, and he immediately picks his phone up, trying her again.

"I'll keep trying, but you need to get going." He lets out a frustrated breath as I hear Roxanne's voicemail pick up once more. "I could try ringing—"

"No!" I snap harshly. "The less contact we have with him now the better. Give Bowser a call and get him to track her phone again. Keep me posted and don't do anything stupid, Zak. Just find her."

Zak raises a questioning brow at me. "You're telling me not to do anything stupid? Okay, man, whatever you say, "he says, bringing the phone to his ear again.

I hear Bowser's gravelly voice come down the line as I leave the kitchen for the front door.

Out in the garage, I bypass my car, deciding that I need something a little more edgy and dangerous tonight.

I throttle it all the way to The Scarlett Door and even run a few red lights. It's a quick journey but long enough for me to come up with a new plan on our deal with Marchant. Parking my bike out the back, I let myself in the back door and run right into Ripley as he's exiting the office.

"Maddox, good timing. Marchant just walked in the door."

I grunt in acknowledgment and follow behind Ripley as we enter the bar. I had hoped the ride over would have calmed me a little, but all it did was generate a nice shot of adrenaline, which is now further fuelling my earlier fiery fury. A fury that has no outlet, and no one target but many.

It's early and the club isn't officially open for another couple of hours, by which time, Marchant will be long gone and so will I.

Candi is at the bar chatting to Lila, while over on the far side, Heather is practicing her routine to some low, sultry number, wrapping her leg around the pole before arching her back toward where her audience will be shortly.

The girls' conversation dies as Ripley and I reach the bar. Lila's eyes subtly flick over my shoulder, no doubt looking for Zak. A spark of disappointment flickers in her eyes momentarily when she realises I'm alone.

The sound of feet shuffling across the floor, several of them, and muted conversation catches my attention as Lila places a drink down on the bar in front of me. I wrap my hand around the glass and turn toward Marchant and his men, leaning casually against the bar.

Sonny Marchant is a young, cocky little shit from Haringay with an overconfident swagger and almost as much gold hanging from his neck as Mr T, which screams look at me, but he's reasonably smart, and *if* he makes it through the next few months, there's a chance he'll make it out the other side.

He laughs at something one of his little lapdogs says, keeping his eyes on me the whole time. His cold, hard stare would be impressive if I was fifteen years younger and trying to work out where I belonged in a world full of gangs and drug lords. But I'm not afraid of Marchant. I'm not afraid of Rogers or Bonner or Laskin.

I've spent my whole life around men like them and guys like Marchant, hell I used to be him.

"Maddox, good to see you again," Marchant greets, turning to Lila and ordering a drink. The fact he doesn't wait for an invitation irks me, but as I said, cocky and overconfident. In his defence, you won't get far in this world without those two traits, however fucking irritating they are.

Once Lila has served them their drinks, I lead them to one of the private rooms. When I reach the first room, I open the door and gesture for Marchant and his guys to enter. I look to Ripley, giving him a nod and holding up three fingers before stepping inside and closing the door. There's a reason why I use this room.

Inside the room, Marchant takes a seat at one end of the curved sofa that surrounds the stripper pole in the centre of the room, while the other two stand at the end.

I sip my drink, my eyes on Marchant the whole time. I've not said a word to him yet, so when he shifts in his chair, I know he's beginning to feel uneasy, and it brings a small smile to my face.

He clears his throat before finally getting to the reason he's here. "Same deal as last time?"

I cross my legs, taking a mouthful of my drink languidly. "No, not this time." He hides his irritation well at the idea I'm about to move the goal posts on him, which I am. "I want you to switch locations."

His eyes narrow, jaw ticking. "To where?"

"I want you to hit up Camden."

His eyes widen. "Are you fucking kidding me? You want me to send my guys to deal right on Rogers' doorstep?"

"No, I'm not *'fucking kidding'*, and yes, that's exactly what you're going to do."

"That wasn't our deal, Maddox." He pauses, weighing up his options. "Okay"—I hear the smaller of Marchant's men give a little gasp—"but I want a bigger cut, both cash and territory."

It's my turn to pause, as though contemplating his terms and placing my drink on the small table at the end of the sofa. When a flash of movement behind Marchant's men catches my eye, I know it's time. "The terms stay the same," I tell Marchant firmly.

His nostrils flare and that tic in his jaw is back. "Then the deal is off." He leans forward, resting a hand on the sofa. "If you think I'm sending my men to their deaths without some sort of compensation, then you're—" His words are cut off as I swipe the arm he's leaning on from under him and clutch his wrist as his head hits the sofa with a dull thud. I place my hand on his head, keeping him in place. There's an audible click that has me raising my eyes and looking down the barrel of a gun.

Lifting my head. I meet the wide, alarmed eyes of a tall, skinny lad with a shaved head.

"Sonny?" the skinny lad pointing the gun at me grits out behind clenched teeth, his hand shaky lightly.

Another click echoes in the frigid silence as I give Sonny's wrist a little twist, causing him to cry out. His eyes flick between me, his mate and my man, who is now standing behind both his men with a gun in each hand and trained on the back of their heads.

"Fuck! Put the fucking gun down, Wes. Jesus Christ," Marchant calls out.

"That's the best idea you've had tonight, Marchant. And I'd hurry up and have your man, Wes, here stand down real fucking sharpish unless he wants a bullet shaped hole in his head."

Wes finally catches on and begins to lower his weapon, but not fast enough for Ripley, who steps forward and cracks him over the head. He goes down like a sack of shit, hitting the floor hard. The gun skitters across the floor out of reach, and Ripley gestures to the other guy to take a seat at the end of the sofa.

"Now, let's try this again, shall we? You will move your dealing to Camden, and you will do it for the same share as before. But as a gesture of goodwill, which your fucking lucky to get after your little buddy here pulled a fucking gun on me, I'll promise not to kill you when I'm finished with you. How does that sound?" When he doesn't answer, I give his wrist another little twist, feeling the bones grind beneath my fingers.

"Ahhh, fuck! Okay, okay."

"Sorry, I couldn't quite hear that? Did you say, *yes, Maddox, thank you, Maddox*"

"Yes, yes. Thank you, Maddox." His voice is laced with pain and muffled from where I'm squashing his face against the soft blood red fabric of the sofa.

"Good. But before I let you get to work, there's a couple more things we need to discuss." Wes groans from his position on the floor as I release Marchant.

He rights himself, straightening his shirt, but keeping his eyes down. "What do you want?" he asks bitterly.

By the time Marchant is leaving, it's been almost an hour and still no word from Zak. I'm at the bar talking to Ripley when Candi strolls over, stepping up beside me.

I ignore her, even when she rests her hand on my thigh and leans in to whisper in my ear.

"You seem a little stressed tonight, Maddox. Maybe there's something I can do to help relax you." She curls herself around me and trails her hand a little higher on my thigh, but before I can stop her, shouting from the back hall draws my attention.

A second later, Roxy bursts into the room, rapidly followed by Zak, who is attempting to grab hold of her. Every eye in the place, turns their way at the exact moment Roxy's eyes land on mine before snapping to Candi beside me.

Chapter Twenty-One

Roxy

DCI Winters sits behind his desk, but it's not him my eyes are focused on. No, my eyes are firmly fixed on the other man, now standing, to the left of me.

"Sir, my apologies, I didn't realise you were busy," I manage to say, peeling my eyes from Noah to look at my DCI. "I can come back later, sir."

"No, no, please, come in and take a seat, Miss Whitmore." Hearing him referring to me as Miss Whitmore smarts more than a little. "Roxanne, I'd like you to meet Noah Shaw, he's an investigator with the National Crime Agency," he says, gesturing to the other seat as Noah and I shake hands, which is a fucking joke. "We were just talking about you actually."

"You were?" I question, eyeing Noah suspiciously.

"Yes, Noah was hoping you'd be able to help him with his current investigation, so your timing couldn't have been better."

"Sir—"

"I'm aware of your current status, Roxanne, but that doesn't affect your duty to aid in the capacity of a member of the general public." His words may have indicated I have a choice, but his tone belies him. Without waiting for my response, he turns to Noah. "If you can give me five minutes with Roxanne, then after that, I'm sure she'll be happy to assist you anyway she can."

Noah, climbs to his feet, reaching across the desk and shaking DCI Winters' hand, thanking him for his time. "I'll wait outside for you, Miss Whitmore," he says, then leaves.

I spend exactly five minutes with the DCI who informs me that while there is no evidence of misconduct on my part, I'll need to wait for the conclusion of the internal investigation before I can be reinstated. If that's what I want.

I don't get a second to let his words sink in or gather my thoughts. As soon as I step out into the hall, Noah is there waiting for me.

I barely look at him as I barge past, seeking out the nearest free interview room. I shove the door open, and as soon as I hear it click shut behind Noah, I round on him.

"What the actual fuck are you doing here? And talking to my DCI...Jesus!"

"Calm down, Roxy. I didn't come here to see you. It was just my cover—"

"Cover? Cover for what, Noah?"

"Another case I'm working, but I was planning to call you when I was done here. We need to talk, Roxy."

My defensive attitude drops a little at his tone and the look on his face. "About what," I ask suspiciously.

"Let's sit," Noah says, gesturing to a chair.

Nobody tells you to sit to give you good news, but I sit all the same, begrudgingly. Noah sits the other side of the table making this feel even more formal. Up until recently, I hadn't sat in this position since I was a teen, but this is the second time in the last few weeks. I can't say I enjoy it.

"What's going on? Is everything okay with the trafficking case?"

"The case is fine. Our little stunt hasn't impacted it at all." He pauses, rubbing a hand over his chin. "How much do you know about the Theo Rogers case?"

My head jerks a little, tilting to the side in confusion. "I wasn't on that case, you know that. Why?" Aside from the fact I wasn't actually here the day Theo was murdered, I deliberately stayed clear of the case for fear of running into Maddox and Zak. Of course, over the years, there have been plenty of cases where our paths could have crossed inadvertently, but there was no way I could have avoided them with Theo's case; there's no way they weren't connected to it in some way or another.

"From an anonymous tip off, we recovered the gun believed to have been used in Theo's murder." He pauses, pulling his phone from his pocket and finding whatever he's looking for before sliding it across the table to me. "Do you recognise this?"

I look down, eyes scanning the picture of a gun. Not just any gun. This particular gun is one I recognise, or at least I'm almost certain it's the same one.

"No, should I?" I ask casually, looking him straight in the eye. Beneath the table, every muscle in my lower body is tensed but above everything is relaxed and masking the fear that's winding through my veins. Because if that is the gun I think it is, then I know without a doubt it belongs to Maddox.

An image of the three us sharpens in my mind; me holding the gun and marvelling at the feel, the power. I'd never even seen a gun until Maddox pulled it out to show me. Hell, I was 15 and even though we lived in an area synonymous with gun crime, the boys tried to keep me away. That's not to say I was an angel, far from it. I remember posing with it and thinking I was some bad arse gangster when in reality I was the severely lacking character foil.

Maddox was on a high that night. I knew that he and Zak

had been spending time with the Rogers family, which wasn't a surprise seeing as Don Rogers was a friend of theirs, so having Theo hand him a gun seemed like a big deal. I didn't really get it then, but I do now.

Noah draws my attention back to him. "According to our anonymous tipper, the gun belongs to Maddox Lawler. But you've never seen this gun before?"

"Come on, Noah, it's not like it's a rare model. In fact, from what I understand, the SIG P210 is very collectible." He raises a curious brow at my show of knowledge. "Don't act so surprised. This particular model was used by the Swiss military for years."

"So, you've never seen this or seen Maddox with this gun?" he pushes, pointing to the picture staring up at me from his phone.

I tilt my head, raising my own eyebrows in condemnation. "No, Noah, I haven't. In case you forgot, the last time I saw the Lawlers, until a few weeks ago, was the night my mum was murdered."

He releases a deep sigh. "You understand why I had to ask?" I nod because I do. I try to ignore the niggling voice at the back of my mind reminding me I just lied to a friend and fellow cop. "It's also been identified as the weapon used in several other murders in the last few years, Roxy, so if you do know anything at all, then you need to tell me." His hesitation picks away at my stern composure, but I hold fast and hold his probing gaze too. "Okay, fine. Another thing I need to talk to you about is Kavanagh."

The subject change, although a small relief, still isn't a topic I'm entirely comfortable with.

"I take it you have some information on him?"

"Yeah, nothing good. The guy has a rap sheet as long as your arm but has always managed to avoid prison for one reason or another."

"Seems prison isn't the only thing he's managed to avoid if you didn't know who he was," I mutter sarcastically.

"Yes, well... Anyway, as the eldest son of the head of the Irish Mob, he's been linked to the the Bratva and obviously Rogers, which alone explains how he's avoided doing time. Dirty money talks, Roxy. You didn't say how you identified him."

"No, I don't plan to either." He begins shaking his head, but I stop him. "Look, I need to be careful what information I give you, Noah. Besides, I'm not a hundred percent certain it was him."

"Roxy, how the fuck am I supposed to explain your intel if you won't tell me how you know this stuff?"

"Not my problem, Noah," I snap, frustrated with his questions and pissed at the knowledge I might have been wrong about Maddox and Zak being the ones to murder Theo. I wanted to talk to him about getting Axel and Eva somewhere safe, but I'm starting to wonder how much I can trust him. That's hard to admit when I've never doubted him before. Maybe I'm being dramatic, over-thinking, or maybe it's because I know he has feelings that go beyond friendship and plain old casual sex. Whatever it is, I need to get the hell out of here. I need air. I need to breathe and sort out what I'm meant to do now.

I rise from my chair, the metal legs scraping against the floor. "I have to go," I say, rushing for the door.

Noah calls after me, but I don't stop. The halls are busy with shift change making it easy for me to disappear.

Bursting out the doors, I suck in a lungful of air like it's my first breath since I stepped inside the station. Hurrying to my car with my head down, I don't see the man up ahead until it's too late.

Something solid hits my shoulder, knocking me off balance. Managing to stay on my feet, my head swivels, and I catch a glimpse of a man I don't recognise. He's not bothered about me seeing him though as he stands there risen to his full height and fists clenched by his side.

"Fucking dirty cop," he spits out, nostrils flaring and eyes wide, burning into me.

I'm just about to respond when Smithy rounds the corner. His eyes scan me before jumping to the guy who looks like he's about to tear into me.

"Hey, what you doing back here?" Smithy calls to him, marching towards us with his hand on his belt ready to draw his baton.

The guy's eyes barely flicker as Smithy draws closer. "Karma is going to fuck you up, bitch!" he snarls, then turns and runs the other way just as Smithy reaches me.

"You okay, Sar...I mean Roxy?"

Turning towards him, I say, "I'm fine, Smithy. He just caught me off guard is all." I don't like that I was so wrapped up in my head I didn't see him. It doesn't scare me. I can take care of myself, but it does make my anger toward Maddox and Zak grow a new head but equally fills me with trepidation about this whole situation.

A hand on my arm snaps me out of my thoughts, and I look to Smithy who has a look of concern on his face.

"You sure you're okay?"

"I'm good, honestly." I give him a playful smile and pat his shoulder as I say, "I need to go. See you later, Smithy, and thanks." I rush off before he can ask anything more, but I hear him call out a bye and take care as I round the corner out of sight.

Once in my car, I drive. No place in mind, just aimlessly driving. I hear my phone ringing, as it has been for the last half hour. Eventually, I park, which is a damn miracle, and walk down to Tower Bridge.

I stop halfway along and look out over the Thames. It's

majestic standing beneath this Victorian suspension bridge, and the view is spectacular. I have a very conflicted history with this bridge.

There have been times, many, when I've stood beneath the historic columns full of happiness and laughter. One particular night that always sticks in my mind is when Maddox and Zak decided to pull a moonie at a passing party boat full of drunken revellers. The gasps of surprise and giggles from the woman below carried all the way to me and reminded me of the scene in the movie *Grease*. We laughed so hard as we ran back across the bridge that my sides hurt. It was also the first time I realised exactly how attracted to them both I was.

They are happy memories, happy times. But there have been others, not so long after that night, that saw me sitting on the railing edge ready to drop to the dark abyss below. Ready to end it all and join my mum and sister. Those were dark days full of raw pain and grief. Full of loss and anger that almost swallowed me whole.

I was always stopped just in time. Sometimes by a passerby, or a car tooting their horn, but on more than one occasion, it was Mitch that turned up. I've never understood how he always managed to find me, but I always assumed it was fate.

Now, I find myself here again. Only this time, I'm not here to end my life, far from it. I don't think I ever really wanted to before. If I had, then I would have found somewhere else to do it, not kept returning to the same place every time. I was just an incredibly sad and lonely messed up teen with a heart left shattered into a thousand pieces and no glue.

My glue had dried up, gone, leaving the pot as arid as the desert.

I found that I didn't need the damn glue. In time, other things, other people, helped rebuild my shattered heart, and I made sure it was strong. So fucking strong.

Not strong enough it seems. I feel the deeply buried

fissures beginning to fracture. I feel the sharp pain piercing my heart every time they are near me, touching me and whispering their devilish desires in my ear. I feel the moment it will split wide open again drawing ever closer, and this time, I know there won't be a damn thing to stop what comes next.

I suddenly feel a presence beside me. It's like my thoughts called him here.

"You and Maddox are lying to me. You're keeping me in the dark, and I don't fucking like it." I turn to look at him.

"Yeah, and you're telling us the whole truth, Rox? Don't be such a hypocrite. Now, let's go before I get a fucking ticket," he snaps, gesturing down the bridge in the opposite direction to where my car is parked.

"Where's Maddox?" I ask.

"He's out, but he'll be home in a while." He holds his hand out, expecting me to take it like we're some loved up couple out for an evening stroll.

I brush his hand aside and start walking in the other direction. "This can't wait. So, where is he, Zak?" He doesn't answer, and I wasn't really expecting him too. "I'll see you at home," I call out behind me, knowing full well his car is parked in the other direction.

I hear him cursing, and when I turn to look, he's jogging away from me. I speed up as I near the end of the bridge and disappear down a side road.

I don't bother trying Rogue first, instead I head straight for The Scarlett Door. The fact Zak wouldn't tell me where Maddox is means it's most likely business, and for that, he'd use their strip club. 'Cause nothing aids a business deal better than booze and sex.

Ignoring the ringing phone in my pocket, I quickly find the place and park in the only other space available at the back of the building. Right next to Maddox's bike.

I take a moment to gather my thoughts. The stop off at

Tower Bridge didn't really do much to calm me. If anything, it only served to remind me of a past best left buried. One that has jumped up and bitch slapped me hard in the face.

Seeing that gun and hearing the confidence in Noah's voice about who the gun belongs to has me worried.

And torn in two.

I climb from the car and reach the rear door just as Zak's car skids into the tiny car park, screeching to a halt behind mine.

I yank the back door open as Zak hollers for me to wait, but I don't listen and step inside. The hall is long with several closed doors along it and dimly lit. The door hasn't even clicked shut when I hear the whoosh of it opening again, forcing me to hurry my steps.

"Rox, stop. Rox!" Zak calls after me.

"No fucking way, Zak. I have questions that need answering. Tonight," I yell back, and a second later, I burst through the doors into the strip club.

Every eye in the room, turns my way, and I feel Zak's fingers brush against my arm, trying to grab hold of me. I take a step out of his reach at the exact moment my eyes land on Maddox. Time seems to stand still as my gaze trails to the woman clinging to his side, her hand on his thigh and a deep look of desire in her eyes.

My spine stiffens, and my fingers curl into fists, forcing my nails to dig into the tender flesh of my palms. I fight the waring desire to turn and run but that's not me.

Heat meets my back, and a hot rush of breath meets my ear. "It's not what you think, Rox." His words blaze a trail of fire down my clammy neck, and again, I step away from him, unable to stand another second in his intoxicating scent.

"Like I give a fuck, Zak." My voice comes out strong, but if you know me, then you wouldn't have missed the small underlying streak of bitterness and bullshit.

Fingertips brush mine, pulling at my clenched fist until I loosen enough for him to slip his hand in mine.

"Come with me," he whispers, tugging on my hand.

I turn away, following Zak back down the corridor we just came from to a door second from the end on the left.

Zak pulls me inside and closes the door behind us. Taking in the room, I see it's an office.

"Rox—"

"It's fine, Zak."

He steps toward me, grasping my hips. "Don't fucking lie, Rox. I felt your reaction."

Looking up at him and leaning in, I say, "Let's get one thing straight, I don't give a shit where Maddox or you stick your dicks." Needing to get away from this conversation and him, I blurt out, "Where's Maddox's gun, Zak?"

His head rears back like I fucking hit him, but he doesn't release me like I hoped. His grip on my hips intensifies almost to the point of pain. "What do you know about it?" he snarls, and if I was anyone else, the dangerous look in his eyes would terrify me. When I don't answer, he forces me to step backward until the backs of my legs meet the desk. "Why the hell are you asking about that? Where did you go today?"

I could break his hold on me in a second, but the fact that I don't, says way too much about how I like it.

"A colleague—"

"The one you've been fucking?" I gasp, and my eyes widen, giving him my answer. "Don't act so surprised, Rox. Mad and I know every man that's ever laid a hand on you, been inside you. You think the infinitesimal amount of jealously you felt at seeing Maddox with Candi even comes close to the jealously that's become a living, breathing thing inside us over the years while we watched you screwing all those guys."

My mind splinters with the revelation they've been

watching me all these years. I can't seem to focus or get any words out as shock and anger whip through me like lightening. When I finally find my voice, it's the anger that wins out.

"You fucking hypocrite! You talk like you and Maddox haven't been fucking your way through London. Haven't been screwing girls two at a time, sharing them, yet you want to call me out on who I fuck. Did you think I'd spend my life like a damn nun? That you ruined me enough to spend my life mourning the loss of a relationship that never was, Zak? Pfft! Well, fuck you." I raise a hand and grip his chin. "I loved every fucking second of it," I say, enunciating every word.

I've been so focused on lashing out at him that I didn't notice one hand had left my hip, so when I release his chin, he pushes me back and steps between my legs as my arse hits the table. I'm about to push back when I feel the sharp point of a blade beneath my chin, and I freeze. Not through fear though. And again, it's a demonstration of my warped mind that I'm turned on by the threat.

I watch as Zak's eyes light with lust, desire and excitement, and a dark smile curls his lips. Keeping the blade at my chin, he leans down.

"Oh, you like this, don't you, Rox?" His lips brush against my own as he speaks, and I almost whimper at the burning need to have his mouth on me.

I'm weak, so fucking weak, when it comes to these two men. Not giving a shit about the blade digging into the soft flesh of my chin or the consequences, I reach forward and nip his bottom lip before sucking it into my mouth. I feel the sting of the blade as it nicks my skin, and I don't care. Our eyes are locked on one another as I release his lip with a pop. Piercing blue pools of liquid heat reach right into the very soul of me a second before his lips slam onto mine. The blade disappears from my chin, clanging to the desk as his hands drop either side of me, caging me in and pushing me down on to the desk.

Our tongues dance with one another, tasting each other, as heat licks at my flesh and between my thighs, causing my clit to throb painfully. Zak breaks the kiss, both of us breathing heavily, and looks down at me.

When he raises his arm, the knife is firmly clenched in his hand, a bead of blood glistening on the tip, then he lowers it to my chest. He traces the blunt edge down between my breasts, nipples hardening instantly, all the way to the waistband of my trousers.

"You like the feel of my blade, Rox." He slips the knife beneath the button of my trousers, and with a flick of his wrist, the button pings off. "How about here, Rox?" he teases, running the back edge of the knife down the seam of my trousers and gliding it over my clit. "Do you want to feel the cold steel of my blade on your pussy, slipping between your wet folds until you come?" The knife glides up and down over my clit a few times, and I'm unable to contain a groan of pleasure as Zak chuckles darkly before pulling away.

Leaning down, he runs his tongue up my neck to my chin, tasting the blood from the small cut there.

"You taste like the sweetest thrill and the darkest sin, and I'm going to enjoy hearing you scream."

Before I can reply or catch my breath, Zak yanks the zip down and tugs at my trousers, tearing them down my body and off my feet. Cold, hard steel meets my naked thigh, and I suck in a breath as he trails it up the inside of my leg. When he reaches the apex of my thighs, I'm wired with anticipation and desperate to feel it run over my clit again, only he skips right past. Taking the edge of my shirt in one hand, he uses the knife to slowly and tortuously pop every button off until he reaches my clavicle. I watch him, fascinated, as the pulse in his neck flutters rapidly, his chest rises with stuttered and restrained breaths, but his eyes—they are the real wonder.

A beautiful and vibrant blue that seem alive, enraptured,

as they follow the knife glancing over my skin. They swirl with each movement, pupils dilating but never eclipsing the colour completely.

I gasp as he cuts my bra clean down the middle, and my breasts spill to the side as it falls away. He's barely touched me, yet I feel like with one single caress or stroke in the right place, I'd explode.

"Fucking beautiful." He leans down, grazing my skin with his lips and every place he touches burns like the hottest fire. When his tongue laves at my nipple, swirling around it, my hips buck, but when he sucks it into his hot mouth and bites down, I almost leap off the desk as a spark of pleasure shoots straight to my pussy.

"Oh fuck," I cry out, unable to contain it any longer. "Zak...I..." My words trail off into nothing more than whimpers as he switches his attention to my other breast. I feel the steel of his knife at my hip, slipping beneath the side of my knickers, and I almost beg him to hurry the fuck up as my body screams for release.

Releasing my nipple with a pop at the same time he slices through my underwear, he takes my mouth, silencing me for a moment.

I hear the rustle of clothing and the clunk of a belt buckle hitting the desk as our tongues war against one another. The sound of metal scraping against wood comes a split second before Zak's fingers delve into my slick folds, grazing over my clit and intermittently dipping in and out of me. His deft fingers make quick work of bringing me to the edge, but just as I'm about to fall, he whispers, "Don't you dare fucking come, Rox, not yet."

"Fuck," I hiss, as he curls his fingers, and it takes everything to hold back my orgasm. "I can't...oh fuck," I pant out.

"When you come, it's going to be over my cock as I fucking own you." Raising up, his free hand skims over my abdomen, my breasts, pinching and tweaking each one, as he continues to finger fuck me relentlessly. His fingers curl again, as he growls, "Eyes on me, Rox. Let me see those eyes as I slide my cock into your sweet pussy." I do as he says, opening my eyes, as he removes his fingers. His eyes are hooded, and desire lights every inch of his face as I feel the head of his cock push at my entrance.

I raise to my elbows to watch as he glides his hand up and down his shaft a couple of times before slowly pushing into me inch by inch. I feel every fucking one as my pussy convulses around him, trying to draw him in further, and my orgasm flutters on the edge again as he bottoms out. His arm snakes around my arched back, raising me up and yanking me to the edge of the desk, arms wrapping around his neck, as he draws back out and thrusts back in with a grunt.

"Fuck me, you feel so fucking good," he grinds out between clenched teeth as his pace picks up, driving in and out. He dips his head, plundering my mouth and swallowing my cry as his hands grasps my arse, squeezing tightly.

Heat flashes across my skin and sweat beads on my forehead as he grinds his hips in the most delicious way, and pleasure coils in my belly. My nails dig into his neck as the first tendrils of my orgasm crest, and I throw my head back, opening my eyes, only to be met with fierce amber ones over Zak's shoulder.

"Fuck...Zak," I pant, unable to form words or stop my orgasm as it crashes over me. I expect to see anger in Maddox's eyes, but instead, there's nothing but pure, unadulterated hunger, and it only makes me come even harder, screaming out Zak's name as he erupts inside me.

My head drops onto my arm, which is still gripped around Zak's neck. "Zak—"

"I know, Rox. It's okay," he whispers breathlessly.

At first, I think he's talking about the sex—the hot

fucking sex—we just had, but then I hear a deep growl from behind as Zak chuckles. His hands reach up and clamp around my face, lifting my head to look at him.

I keep my eyes closed afraid to open them, afraid of what I'll see. Lips ghost across mine before his hands fall away, and I feel the loss of him as he moves away, only to be replaced by the heat and hands of another a second later.

"Tinks." Maddox's nickname for me rumbles up his throat in a deep growl, and I flinch as he swipes a thumb over my bottom lip. "Open your fucking eyes."

The order has the desired effect, and my eyes snap open, glaring at him scornfully. He smiles, and it's full of accomplishment. "You proud of your-fucking-selves, huh? You want me to leave you alone so you can compare notes and brag about who gave me the best orgasm? Well—" His lips meet mine, cutting me off, and I stiffen in his arms.

My mind scrambles to make sense of what just happened. I can't breathe, I can't think, I can't help the jolt of pleasure zipping through me as his tongue demands entry.

When he breaks the kiss a moment later, I feel wrung out. I feel exhausted. I feel like I'm swimming against the tide and carrying the weight of two men on my back who are slowly drowning me.

"Watching you just now has me hard as fucking stone. But next time, they'll be no watching, Tinks. Next time, you're going to ride my cock while Zak fucks your dirty little mouth, and you'll come so hard, you'll see fucking stars. You understand?"

I nod, shocking the shit out myself when his words finally make it to my brain and register what I agreed to. I see Zak out the corner of my eye, back against the wall, his head is dipped down, but I see the smirk creasing one side of his face. Everything about his body language tells me what Maddox just suggested turns him on, as evidenced by the bulge in his trousers despite just being buried inside me.

Maddox kisses my forehead before turning and walking away, leaving the two of us alone again.

"Uh, I...er." I shake my head to clear the fog and try again to make my mouth work. "I need to use the bathroom." The words come out clear, but they're monotone and emotionless.

I slide from the desk and attempt to straighten my clothes, but there's really no point. My bra and shirt are beyond saving, and when I get my trousers on, sans underwear, I can't do them up.

A shadow falls over me as I attempt to make some sort of makeshift top with what's left of my shirt.

"Here, put this on." Zak holds a t-shirt out to me. I take it without looking at him and quickly throw it over my head, eager to cover myself.

I pull it down, stopping mid-thigh. The scent that envelops me, tells me it's Maddox's, and I resist the urge to bring it to my nose and inhale it. There is something seriously wrong with me. I just had sex with Zak while Maddox, his brother and the man I fucked the other night, watched.

A finger beneath my chin, lifts my head.

"Don't over think it, Rox. This is right. You are right. I know there are a lot of things we need to talk about, things you need to know, and you'll get the answers. For now, let your body and heart do the talking." He drops a sweet and delicate kiss on my lips before taking my hand and leading me to a toilet down the hall.

Chapter Twenty Two

Zak

I leave Rox to clean up, telling her to wait for me in the office when she's done. I should be grinning like the damn Cheshire cat right now, but my gut churns with worry. Things are happening fast and not exactly to plan. Maddox and I knew the gun would be an issue, but we were hoping to have a little more time first. She doesn't trust us, and that's a huge fucking problem.

Her lack of trust isn't without cause, and this shit with the gun isn't going to make gaining it back any fucking easier. How do you convince the person who trusted you exclusively for four years to trust you again after you promised to always be there, then walked away at the worst time in their life? And Roxy isn't your average person. She can hold a grudge better than anyone.

When I push through the bar door, Maddox is deep in conversation with Ripley. Making my way over, Ripley places a shot of my favourite whiskey on the counter before walking down the bar.

"Where is she?" he asks, taking a sip of his own drink.

"In the toilet out back. I told her to wait for me in the

office, but I doubt she will. She's spooked, Mad, and not only about what just went down."

"What do you mean?"

I sigh. "I found her at Tower Bridge." His head snaps in my direction, a concerned frown pulling at his brows. "She was just looking out over the water this time, but for her to go there... She asked about the gun," I tell him.

"Why the fuck would she ask..." His words trail off as he figures it out. "Noah." I nod. "What did you tell her?"

"Nothing. We kind of got distracted. But you know she's going to want answers soon. We need to tell her before someone else does. And if Noah is already digging around, then it means they have it."

"They've got fuck all. It's why he's bringing it to her. Telling her could be a mistake, but we don't have a choice now." He finishes his drink, slamming his glass down. "Ripley heard it was the Acers that shot up the club, but there's no way they did it without help. The bigger question is was it Bonner or Rogers?"

"But isn't that where the tip off about Laskin dealing on our patch came from, Ripley's mate on the inside?"

"Yeah, it is. Ripley's wary about the whole thing and thinks maybe it was all part of the same ruse. He's guessing they were hoping we'd both be there and could take us out together in one fell swoop."

"And his mate?"

"Dead. He found out yesterday from the guy's sister."

"Fuck!"

"Let's get the fuck out of here. The deal with Marchant is done, and we need to get Rox home and out of sight."

I finish my drink, sliding my glass on to the bar next to Maddox's, and follow him out.

As I suspected she's not in the toilet or the office, and

when we reach the car park it's not her car that's missing but mine.

Maddox laughs as he strides to his bike. "Guess you're walking home, Zee, unless you've got her keys."

"Funny fucker. How are you laughing about this?"

He swings his leg over his bike, and says, "She's in your car, right?" I nod. "So, we don't need to worry about finding her this time." He pulls his helmet down over his head and starts the engine, revving it before peeling away and leaving me standing there.

Pulling my phone from my pocket, I open the tracking app. I'm surprised to see she's headed for the house, and I quickly order an uber.

Back at the house, I find Maddox in the kitchen tucking into a bowl of pasta and drinking a beer.

"Where is she?"

Maddox swallows his mouthful and washes it down with a swig of beer. "In her room making a call apparently."

"So, you haven't spoken to her yet?"

"Nope." He delivers the one-word answer with a pop of the 'p' before shoving another forkful of pasta into his mouth.

I drop down on a stool and watch him knowing how much it will piss him off.

"Stop fucking staring," he snaps, not less than two minutes later, and I laugh.

We don't usually talk feelings and shit, but there have been a few occasions when it's been necessary. Most of them surrounding Rox.

We dragged her into our world the first time we met her, and ever since then, we've been protecting her. Silly really considering what she needed protecting from the most was us.

I wasn't lying earlier when I told her that we know every man that's ever laid a finger on her, platonically or intimately. Some of them are no longer breathing. Right about now, I imagine she's upstairs pacing the floor and trying to figure out what the hell is happening with us all or on the phone to Jess.

Yeah, we know who Jess is and her fiancé, Rick Sullivan, too. We owe a big thanks to Triple R Security for getting rid of Sean Donovan. It's just a shame that Rogers was all too eager to step in where Donovan left off.

Rox's recent human trafficking ring bust has meant a halt on the majority of trafficking, for now at least.

Pushing his plate away, Maddox stands. "That's it, she's had enough time." He turns to leave but stops, and I spin my head to see why.

Rox is standing in the doorway with the ends of her hair damp from the shower and wearing fresh clothes.

"Let's talk," she demands, turning and striding toward the lounge. "I'll have a beer, please," she adds, disappearing round the corner into the lounge, which we hardly ever use.

Maddox follows, calling out to me as he goes, "Make that two, Zak." His laughter rings out as I slide off the stool and grab three beers from the fridge.

I've no idea how much Maddox is willing to tell her, so I'll do my usual and sit, watch and wait.

Stepping into the lounge, Maddox has taken the armchair, elbows on his knees and hands dangling between his parted legs looking somewhat agitated, while Rox has taken residence in the far corner of the sofa and leaving me no option but to sit on the other end from her.

I hold out Maddox's beer to him then hand one to Rox before sitting.

Maddox wastes no time in throwing the ball firmly in her court. "What do you want to know?" It's a good tactic.

Rox sips her beer, watching him carefully. "How about you start with the real reason why I'm here, Maddox?"

"Already given you a reason. We need your help to bring Rogers down."

"Yeah, I'd believe that if it wasn't for the fact since I agreed to help you've not mentioned Rogers once. I don't appreciate being taken for a ride, Maddox. You're not telling me everything. Correction, you're not telling me fuck all."

Maddox twirls the bottle loosely hanging from his fingertips as he watches her. I see the cogs turning and determining how much to tell her.

"How much do you know about Rogers."

Rox shakes her head. "No, Maddox, you tell me what you have and how you think it's going to bring down a family that's ruled parts of these streets since Madonna tried to convince us all she was a fucking virgin." There's a heavy silence before Rox speaks again. "Look, until you tell me what's going on, I can't help you. Or was Rogers just a rouse so you could mess with my life and fuck me?"

Maddox lets out a low growl. "If that was true, it's a lot of fucking trouble to go to just for a taste of your pussy. Don't get me wrong, it's good pussy, but I don't need some elaborate story to fuck you." Rox rolls her eyes at Maddox and his giant ego, not letting his words bother her in the slightest. "Rogers murdered his father, and, no, I don't have evidence, but he's trying to frame us for it."

"Yes, yes, tell me something I don't already know, Maddox. Like how the fuck the gun that killed Theo looks just like yours and how the cops have it? Tell me that." Rox looks between us, but neither of us looks at the other. "Did you do it?"

Both of us snap our heads up to look at her, but Maddox answers her before me.

"Fuck no! Regardless of who Theo was or what he did, he

was like a damn father to us. We fell out, yes, but murder him? No, Roxanne, not even if my life depended on it." I watch him closely, knowing what he daren't say. But I know Rox's next words even before she opens her mouth.

"How about Zak's life or mine?"

Maddox leans further forward, shuffling to the edge of the seat. Face a mask of indifference and truth, but I know better.

"Not even then." His voice doesn't waiver, and his tone is void of any emotion. This is what my brother does with so much ease. He is an empty vessel when the time calls for it. I can't imagine how bitter the words taste on his tongue because they scorch a path through my mind just hearing them. And we both know that there's no truth in them. He would rip the world apart for me, so for Rox? Hell would be a safer place to be if her life was in danger.

If she's affected by his lack of emotion, she doesn't show it. I didn't expect anything else. If there's one thing Maddox and I have learnt about Rox over the last ten years, it's that she can switch her emotions off too and to great effect.

"Why would he murder his own father? And why would he frame you two?"

"Aside from the most obvious answer, that's a long story, and one I don't have time to go into at the moment. If the police have the murder weapon, then Rogers is upping the ante."

"Okay, hold on, what does any of this have to do with me? Aside from the fact I'm no longer a cop, and even if I was, I'm not sure what you thought I'd be able to do, I don't have anything to do with this. Like I've not seen Rogers for almost as long as you two, and I've gone out of my way to avoid the guy." Rox's demeanour flickers, and I catch the tail end of a tremor through her body.

She's hiding something. At least she thinks she is. Unfortunately, the very thing she's keeping to herself is, in part, what instigated this long running feud between us and Rogers. Rox has no idea that we already know what happened between her and Rogers, and we are even more aware of the fallout of their confrontation.

My eyes catch Maddox's as I see him battling with what to say. Whatever answer he gives her now will be a half truth, and one that will come back around like a damn boomerang later, or it could change the next course of events before we are ready.

Fuck! I hate lying to her, but I give Maddox a look that without words perfectly expresses my answer.

"We think he's after you." Maddox doesn't sugar coat it in any way.

Her head jolts back in surprise. "What? Why? I don't understand."

"We don't know, Rox. We are as surprised as you and trying to figure this out," I tell her.

She turns to look at me, eyes assessing and wary, as they should be. I'd swear on my own life she knows we aren't telling her the whole truth. But she's not ready for the fucked up, twisted truth that explains Rogers reasons for marking her, and us, with a target in this war he's waging on London.

"Bullshit!" she snaps. "You know, or you have an idea, so why keep it from me?"

I shake my head but hold her stare. "It's not that simple. You just have to—"

"Trust you, right?" I nod, aware that she doesn't and isn't likely to any time soon. But if we are going to stop Rogers and keep Rox alive then she needs to, which is why, for now, she has to remain in the dark. "You want me to trust you, yeah?" I nod again. "Then you're going to do something for me that will go some way to earning you that trust."

I already have an inkling as to what that favour is, and she looks to Maddox as she talks.

"Axel and Eva, I want them moved to safety, and I want your word that no harm will come to them."

Maddox's eyes light with fire at the thought of letting Axel free and not ending his life like we've always been taught to do. Theo's voice rings in my head as if he were standing right beside me *'never allow a traitor to breathe the same air as you once they have shown their true colours'*. I wonder if he'd still stand by that if he were alive to see what his son is doing and how he's betrayed his own father. But then I guess it wouldn't really surprise him given we are in this situation because of a betrayal that cost the life of one innocent and nearly another already.

Even criminals have a moral code they live by. Of course, it varies from culture to culture, but no matter what that code is, once you cross it you can't come back from it, and it doesn't matter who you are, who you're related to, the code stands. The fact that Rogers pissed all over that moral code ten years ago because of his own sick and twisted desires and again three years ago when he murdered his father, means he's living on borrowed time.

Rox waits patiently for Maddox to give his answer. It's almost like she knows how hard this is for him.

"What do you have in mind?" he asks, his voice strained.

"I need to make a call first, if you agree."

"Witness protection?" he queries with a raised brow.

"No, not now," she states, her voice quietening, and a small frown drawing her brows together. I'm surprised given what she said earlier. I'm guessing something or someone has made her change her mind. "I have a friend that might be able to help."

Sullivan. Why am I not surprised.

Maddox looks to me briefly, and I shrug.

"Fine. Are you going to tell me why Eva is so important to you?"

"No, I'm not," she says matter of fact. "Comes down to trust, Maddox. And right now, it's not even in the top hundred on the scale of how much I trust you both."

He doesn't push her knowing there's no point. At this stage, we are in a tug-o-war that's reached a stalemate, and until someone gains an edge, we aren't going anywhere.

We sit in silence while we all drink our beers. It's not awkward, it's not strained, it's quietly comfortable, which is strange given what went down between us today.

Rox seems somewhat relaxed, and I'm not sure if that's a good or bad thing. I can't read her though, not like I used to be able to and that hurts.

We've watched her over the years, not twenty-four seven, but there's always been eyes on her. Eyes that were welcome. Eyes that were allowed to see inside her soul when she was hurt, upset, happy and everything in between.

There is so much more to come. There is so much hurt coming her way, and it eats away at me like nothing else.

Maddox and I never wanted to be the cause of her pain. We never imagined that the small twelve-year-old girl we saw that day would ever come to mean so much to us. I don't think we even realised it until it was almost too late. I don't think Rox knows it even now. But she will. When the time is right, she'll learn the truth of everything. What comes after? Only the fates know the answer to that.

Chapter Twenty-Three

Roxy

A s I sit in this lounge watching Maddox and Zak, all I can think about is how I got back here. I don't remember the drive back to this house. My mind was somewhere else entirely. It was back in that office at The Scarlett Door. It was...lost. When I think about it, my mind, and even my soul, have been lost since the night that changed everything.

Before my world fell apart, I'd dreamed about what it would be like to give my body to Maddox and Zak, even brought myself to orgasm while whispering their names into the darkness of my room. But, in reality, it was something I believed would never come to pass. A silly girl's fantasy. Something, I now know, many women imagine.

After they betrayed me and having finally accepted it, I turned off every emotion they ever raised in me. I focused on myself and my career. Relationships were never going to be my thing, not in the traditional sense anyway. The one and only relationship my mother ever had was with drugs and alcohol by the end. Tracey Parks' relationship with men was almost non-existent after James Whitmore. She learned her lesson the hard way. Falling for a married man and getting pregnant only to discover he was touched by the devil and that she was nothing more than a good time leaves an lasting mark on a person. Having that same person discover you had that child against his wishes and come for you in a way that guaranteed your destruction really couldn't have ended any other way. As for the father of my sister, I've no clue. She never mentioned him, and I don't remember another man in her life before Star came along, or even after until the dealers and punters began traipsing through the door.

Now, I find myself at an impasse. I know, without asking the question, that if I follow this path I seem to be winding down it can only end in disaster. The Lawler brothers will ruin me. The question is am I prepared? Is it what I want?

The knock of glass on wood snaps me out of my thoughts, and I look up to see Maddox tapping the rim of his bottle, which appears to be empty, on the side of the table.

"What's happening with your house?" Maddox asks, throwing me a little.

"You mean you don't know? Now that's a disappointment," I retort with equal amounts sarcasm and surprise.

He chuckles, shaking his head. "No, Roxanne, I don't know on this occasion. Why don't you enlighten me."

The sofa shifts as Zak rises to his feet, leaning forward to take the empty bottle from Maddox's fingers and holding out a hand toward mine. "Another?" he asks.

I quickly drink what's left and hand the bottle to him. His fingers brush mine as he takes it, lingering a second longer than necessary. A spark ripples along my arm as I pull away, and I see a knowing smirk pull at the corner of Zak's mouth.

"Sure," I reply, shuffling back and tucking my legs beneath me. My eyes follow him as he leaves, trailing down his body as my tongue swipes out to wet my dry lips.

As he disappears out of sight, I turn back to find Maddox grinning at me. The smile I didn't even know I was wearing slides off my face at getting caught checking Zak out. And this feeling right now is another issue with what happened between me and each of these two men. Brothers, not by blood, nonetheless. Blood doesn't always make a family.

Attempting to gloss over my blatant staring at Zak, I answer Maddox's original question.

"I'm waiting for the final report, but—"

"You don't need to hide it, you know?" Maddox cuts me off, and at the confused look on my face, he continues, "There's nothing to be embarrassed about, Roxanne."

I'm not ready for this conversation. "I need to go make a phone call. I'll see you later," I tell him, rising to my feet. As I do, I'm met with a hard wall of muscle blocking my way. My breath stutters in my lungs, and my skin heats at the closeness of him. Before I have a chance to move back, Maddox reaches out, tucking my hair behind my ear. As his finger brushes the shell of my ear, he continues, trailing it all the way down, over the pulse in my neck and across until he reaches my chin. With gentle pressure, he lifts my face up so that I'm looking right at him.

He steps impossibly closer, and this time my breath doesn't stutter but ceases altogether as he dips his head and brings his lips to mine with the barest touch. It's a mere second that feels like an eternity before he deepens the kiss, and I fall.

I hear the faint clinking of glass, but it's eclipsed as Maddox's hand grasps my nape, gripping me tight and holding me there. His tongue delves into my mouth, and the sweet taste that is uniquely him along with the bitter tang of beer elicits a groan.

Hands grip my hips, and it takes me a second to realise they aren't Maddox's. They slide up my torso, fingers skimming over my breasts before working their way back down and across my stomach.

As Maddox continues to possess my mouth, a second set of lips meet my neck, laving at my skin, teeth grazing over the tender junction between my neck and shoulder.

I feel hands all over my body, and the unmistakable feel of Zak's erection grinding into my arse.

My head drops back, breaking the kiss and resting on the shoulder behind me as Maddox trails a path down my neck with his lips. Hands inside my t-shirt, push it up and over my breasts, revealing them to Maddox who eagerly takes a nipple into his mouth, and my back arches, pitching my pelvis forward where I feel Maddox's hard length brush against my core. It's the smallest touch, yet it builds an immense desire for more.

A hand slips beneath the waistband of my joggers, searing over my skin on its path to my pussy and draws a growl of approval from Zak when he finds me bare.

"Fuck, Rox, you're drenched," he groans, dipping a finger between my folds and circling my clit before easily pushing two fingers inside. He curls them just as Maddox's teeth graze my nipple, sending a jolt of pleasure-pain through me. I turn my head, breath ghosting over my lips a second before Zak takes my mouth.

The taste of him on my tongue collides with the taste of Maddox from minutes before. It's erotic and so fucking hot. But then the reality of what I'm doing pops like a confetti filled balloon in my lust crazed mind as hands begin to slide my joggers down over my hips.

"Stop," I whisper, but it comes out breathy, not at all how I had intended thanks to Zak's continued assault on my pussy. My body completely at odds with my mind.

Blocking out the screaming, wanton whore that's taken residence in my head, I make a grab for my joggers just as Maddox continues to slide them down my legs. This time when I speak, it comes out firmer.

"Stop. Stop." I pull away, pushing Zak back so I can escape the heady and intoxicating pull of them both. Stepping aside, I right my clothes, covering myself, as I put more space between us. "I can't do this." I say, moving further away from them and their wide-eyed looks. "God, what am I doing?"

"Rox, it's—"

I shake my head. "No! Don't say it's okay, Zak. It's so not." I look to Maddox as he stands with his hands at his sides. His fists twitch, and the veins on his arms pop with each movement. Fuck, I must be out of my freaking mind to have stopped what was happening. My eyes flick back to Zak as he moves a step closer. I take a step back, putting my hand up to stop his advance. "Don't, please." I ignore the worried look in his eyes and quickly leave the room.

In my room, I collapse on the bed, burying my head in the covers to hide my cries of frustration. There are no tears, just venting.

Sufficiently purged of my annoyance, I sit up and snatch my phone from the bedside table where I'd left it charging.

I take a couple of deep breaths to centre myself as I pull up the number. Once I'm certain I can speak to her without breaking apart, I hit call.

"Rox? You okay?"

I swallow down the instantaneous lump that forms in my throat at the sound of her voice and force words out through the narrowed space. "I'm okay. Look, I need your help. Well, actually, Rick's help too."

"First off, I call bullshit on the *'I'm okay'* line you just spun me. But it's fine, I'll see for myself when I get there. Now, tell me what you need?"

I give Jess a brief overview of what I need. During which I realise that we need to check on Eva.

Once I'm done, Jess tells me that her and Rick will be here tomorrow. She doesn't try to pry any further information out of me, but I know once she gets here tomorrow, there will be no escaping her interrogation.

Ending the call, I check the time to see it's late, and there's probably not much I can do about Eva tonight. Then I wonder if anyone has checked on Axel.

Chucking my phone on the bed, I metaphorically suit up as I exit my room. The house is quiet as I descend the stairs, and I hope the guys have gone to bed.

I hurry to the kitchen and the door to the cellar when it becomes obvious there is no one else up. A chill ripples across my skin as I reach the bottom of the cellar stairs.

I unlock Axel's door and step inside unsure of what I'll find. Thankfully, I find him laid out on a small camping bed that wasn't here before.

He looks as though he's asleep, but I know better. I take a few steps toward him and watch the small increase in his breathing. I bet it's killing him to remain still and keep up the pretence when he has no idea who is here.

"You can stop with the pretending to sleep, Axel. I'm not fooled." His eyes flicker behind closed lids at my voice while he takes a minute to decide whether to give up or not.

His face is clean, and he has some clothes on too. I guess this room is no longer a death sentence waiting to happen and more a necessity to keep him alive. I have no doubt that Axel is on Rogers' hit list. The thought has my earlier thread of concern for Eva doubling. Shit!

"How long have you been here, Axel?" I ask.

"Too fucking long. What do you want, *Roxy*?"

"I'm not the enemy, Axel. How long?"

"I don't fucking know. Maybe four days. Getting your arse beat is not conductive to time keeping or memory."

I consider the timeline along with what Axel told us about how he ended up at the door of Rogue the morning after the shooting. He believes his initial beating came at the hand of

Rogers' men, but he doesn't understand why given he'd done everything Rogers asked of him. Something else must be at play here.

I turn away as my concern for Eva's safety tugs at me.

"Hey, what's going on?" I ignore him, even when I hear him shuffling from the bed and padding after me. "Roxy, what the fuck's going on?" His hand my arm, pulls me back to face him.

"Hands off, Axel," I tell him with a scowl, pulling my arm back from him. "I need to check something. I'll be back later." I begin walking away again.

"Roxy," he calls to me, and something in the tone of his voice has me pausing and turning to him. "I don't give a fuck what happens to me, but please don't let them hurt her." I give a nod and leave, closing and locking the door behind me.

Back upstairs, I hurry to dress, grabbing my phone and sneaking back downstairs. I don't have my car, but I never returned Zak's keys after stealing his car back at the strip club.

Climbing in, I consider whether I should have woken one of them, but I quickly dismiss the idea when an image of what happens when I'm with them flashes through my mind. It seems spending time either alone or together with them doesn't make an ounce of difference, my body betrays me anyway.

The streets are quiet at this time of night, and I make it to Eva's Camden home in no time. I switch the engine off and watch and wait for five minutes before climbing from my car. The house appears quiet. But appearances can be deceiving. A lesson I've learnt a time or two over the years, and one I now heed.

I may know who she is, but chances are, she won't know me. As I climb the long stone steps to her front door, I consider exactly what I'm going to say. Regardless, knocking on her door at this ridiculous hour is never going to go down well.

Reaching the door, I press the bell for her apartment, hearing the ding dong echo inside, and wait. I'm just about to ring again when I hear a noise just beyond the door. The click of a catch being unlocked sounds a second before the door opens. The door chain prevents the door opening any further, and I'm thankful she's sensible enough to have it in place.

Two hazel eyes shadowed by darkness peer out at me. "Can I help you?" she asks warily, but I see recognition in her eyes.

"Eva?" She nods. "I'm sorry to trouble you at this late hour, but I wondered if we could talk." It's lame, but a small shuffle from behind the door has me on alert.

I see a wince before she speaks again, and I'm almost certain she's not alone. "No, I'm sorry. I can't help you." Her eyes widen on the word help like she's trying to tell me something. She starts to close the door, and I know if I don't do something to stop her my opportunity to get her out will be lost.

Aware that this is a dangerous game but confident it will work, I say, "I know where he is." The words hang in the air for a moment as her eyes narrow coldly. What I can see of her face tells me she's not happy I'm giving Axel up, but it's the only way to get inside.

She closes the door, leaving me to think I misjudged whoever is behind the door with her, but then I hear the rattle of the chain as she slides it off, and the door opens again, wider this time, permitting me access.

I'm not even going to pretend I don't know this was a stupid idea. I have no weapon, and no one knows I'm here. *Real smart, Rox.*

As I step over the threshold, I consider shoving the door back into the arsehole behind it, but I'm guessing he has a gun or knife pointed at Eva. I step further inside, and Eva moves to the side allowing me in. A glint of silver in the faint light gives me my answer and knowing that once I'm inside and the door is closed it's going to be incredibly hard to get out again, I take my chances.

On my next step, I stumble, and Eva's hand shoots out to catch me, bringing us closer together. Gripping her arm, I whisper, "Run." At the same time, I pull my arm back, yanking Eva forward toward the exit as I give the door a hard shove and hear a grunt as it smacks into the guy behind it.

"Move. Get in the car," I tell her, pushing all my weight on the door to hold him in place, hopefully long enough for Eva to reach the car. She doesn't argue and races down the stone steps to the path.

"You stupid bitch! You're going to pay for this," he growls out between clenched teeth as he begins to push back. He swipes out with the hand holding the knife, catching me on the arm, and I hiss as it slices through my flesh. With no time to worry about it, I look back to Eva and see her climbing into the passenger side of the car as my feet begin to slide on the hall floor. As he puts his whole weight on the door, I twist my body round so my back is to the door before jumping away and leaping down the steps two at a time.

I hear a chorus of curses a second before the front door slams closed. I have my keys ready and am in the car starting the engine just as the front door swings open revealing a guy with a murderous look on his face. He barrels down the steps, and I pull away from the curb a split second before he reaches us.

I watch in the rear-view mirror as he pulls his phone from his pocket and brings it to his ear as I turn at the end of the street.

I take a quick glance to Eva beside me to see her with her arms wrapped around her waist.

"Eva, you okay?"

She spins her head, eyes pinned on the side of my face as I watch the road. "Am I okay?" she asks slow and precise like I don't understand English. "Oh, yeah, I'm just fucking peachy. I love being held hostage for two days, then dragged from my house in the middle of the night by a corrupt cop." She blows out a breath and folds her arms rather than hugging herself.

I don't say anything more, and we ride in silence for a bit. Warmth trickles down the inside sleeve of my jumper and with each flex of my bicep the slice on my arm stings. That is until the rumble of a bike engine draws my attention to the rear-view mirror.

"Perfect," I mutter, realising who it is. Eva twists in her seat to get a look behind us.

"Who is that?"

"You don't know?" I ask, a little surprised by that revelation. I see her shake her head. "Well, shit. This is going be all kinds of fucked up fun then."

"What does that mean, and where are we going?"

"You'll see soon enough," I reply, turning down the road to Maddox's house. He follows close behind, revving the engine like he wants to ram me in the arse. I almost choke on the irony of that thought.

He's pissed! But I have something to deflect from the fact I snuck out of the house and have now brought Eva to theirs without asking.

Chapter Twenty Four

Maddox

My bike skids, kicking up gravel, as I pull alongside Zak's car in the driveway. I barely get the stand in place before I'm off my bike, ripping the helmet from my head and dumping it on the seat, then marching toward her as she steps from the car.

I open my mouth to go in on her, but she holds a hand up and beats me to it. "Do not even start with me, Maddox. I'm not in the mood." The sound of more feet crunching across the gravel has me looking over the top of the car to see Zak heading this way.

A head of brown hair appears from the other side of the car, and I realise that it's Eva. Jesus fucking Christ.

"You've got to be fucking kidding me, Roxanne!"

Rounding on me, her finger in a severe point, she says, "Not bloody kidding, and you're going to want to hear who I bumped into at her house too. You want to do this standing here or inside?"

Roxanne doesn't wait for an answer, but instead she strides to Eva, who she says a few words to before walking to the house with Eva following.

Zak waits for me, and we head into the house together just as Roxanne and Eva disappear up the stairs.

I stand at the bottom until long after they've gone. Zak has walked off to the kitchen, and I can hear him in the fridge.

When I finally join him, he's making a sandwich from left over chicken.

"Want one?" he mumbles around a mouthful.

I shake my head. I don't know how he manages to eat at this time of night. I'd be up all night with indigestion. I ignore the annoying little fucker in my head telling me it's because I'm an old man. I don't need a reminder. I feel every damn one of my twenty-nine years. The last ten have aged me, yet my life expectancy has lowered considerably.

"Spit it out, Mad. I can see the words forming in your mind, so just say them."

I swipe a hand down my face, stopping to scratch at the stubble on my chin. "You sound just like her when you say shit like that, you know." He shrugs, and I continue, "What the fuck was she thinking bringing Eva here? That there was going to be some happy fucking reunion or some shit?"

"Nah, she's just being Rox, man. Isn't that why we—" His words cut off at the sound of footsteps in the hall.

A second later Roxanne comes into view carrying a pillow.

"Is this a welcoming committee or a lynch mob? Either way, I'm too tired for this shit." She dumps the pillow on the counter before grabbing a glass from the cupboard and filling it with water.

I watch as she drinks down the whole glass before refilling it. She strides past me, flicking out a hand to grab the pillow as she goes, but I throw out my own hand, clutching hold of her arm and stopping her.

She sucks in a sharp breath at my touch, and the glass falls from her hand, shattering in a spray of cold water and glass, and her fingers grip mine, which are wrapped around her arm, trying to pry them away.

"Shit!" she curses, as I release her. My fingers come away wet, and when I look down, they are covered in blood.

"What the fuck, Roxanne!" I snatch the pillow from her other hand, tossing it aside.

"Hey, I need that!"

Before she can say anything more, I reach forward and pick her up, placing her on the counter as Zak drops the first aid kit beside her.

"Why the hell didn't you tell me you were hurt?"

"Aww, are we going to play doctors and nurses now, Maddox?" Her words are laced with sarcasm, and she even tilts her head, offering me an exaggerated grin. I ignore her, and instead I tug at her jumper while Zak begins clearing up the glass and water on the floor.

Easing it over her head, which she allows, surprisingly, I get a look at the cause of her bleeding.

"Ooh, that's pretty," she says, her eyes raking over the gash to her bicep as I reach for the first aid kit.

"Do you think this is funny?" I snap, pinning her with narrowed eyes and a deep frown.

"Not particularly." She shrugs nonchalantly. "But it's okay. Dr. Mad is here to fix me. Isn't that right? Oh, but I must be confused." She brings a finger to her mouth, pouting her lips, and looks to the ceiling as though thinking. Bringing her eyes back to me, her nostrils flare as she says, "Because you're only good at breaking things." Her tone is challenging and full of venom.

I'm not entirely sure how or when, but I find my hand wrapped around her throat, holding her an inch from my face. I see a sliver of fear as I stare into her baby blues.

"Breaking things is what I do best, Roxanne. There's only

one thing in this world that I've regretted breaking, and I always intended to fix her again." My fingers flex against her neck, and I feel the rapid thrum of her pulse beneath them.

"I do—"

I cut her off, slamming my lips to hers. The move is two-fold. Shutting her up, but also stopping words I'm not ready to say yet spilling from my mouth. I allow myself a minute to take from her, and the slight shift of her body tells me she might be mad as hell but can't help herself any more than I can.

A growl from behind has me pulling back, my hand still gripped tightly around her neck. Her eyes are closed, and she looks at peace and free from pain.

The moment shatters the second her eyes open and all the hurt, pain and confusion floods back into her. No matter how much I want to take it all away again, I can't yet.

I let her go, taking a small step back so we aren't touching. Now is not the time. She's injured. I might not be able to fix everything else right now, but I can fix this.

I drop my eyes from hers and drag the first aid kit across the top towards me. Zak places a bottle of whiskey beside it. I snatch it up, opening the lid and handing it to Roxanne. She takes it, looking up at me from downcast eyes and swollen lips that are just begging for me to take again.

"Drink," I tell her. She glugs mouthfuls of the whiskey between hisses as I clean her wound. Thankfully, it's not too deep, and after a couple of Steri-Strips and a dressing, she's all good.

"What happened, Rox," Zak asks, while I pack away, taking the bottle of whiskey back from her.

She lets out a heavy sigh and rests her hands on the edge of the counter. "I made a call to my friend, but it got me thinking about whether anyone had checked on Eva. I got a feeling as soon as she opened the door that she wasn't alone and not through choice. It seems that your little friend from Oxford Street got there before us," she says, looking directly to Zak.

"Tommy?"

"Yeah, Tommy Evans."

"Hold on a second, you know who he is?" I ask.

"I didn't get a proper look at him before, but I did last night. I know him and his brother, Sammy, and have arrested them a couple of times. But Tommy and Sammy have never been aligned with one single organisation before, so why the hell was Tommy wearing Bonner's colours the other day but clearly doing Rogers' dirty work last night?"

"Yeah, well, it looks like they finally made their choice. Tommy's been a dead man walking since he tipped Rogers off a couple of weeks ago, and as for Sammy...well, he's already pushing up daisies," I confess.

Roxanne eyes me, and I can see the burning question behind her eyes.

"No, Roxanne, I didn't fucking kill him. Not directly, anyway."

"What the hell does that mean? Do I even want to know?"

"Let's just say that Sammy made the perfect message from Rogers about what happens to people who fuck with him."

"Jesus Christ, Maddox." She shakes her head and jumps down from the counter. "My friends will be here tomorrow to collect Eva and Axel. I need some sleep." She snags the pillow from the counter as she heads back out into the hallway to the lounge.

"Looks like we'll have a house full tomorrow. Should be fun," Zak jokes as he heads to bed too.

I lean forward, resting my hands on the counter and dropping my head. I take a few deep breaths. Being around Roxanne is like having every wound ever inflicted upon me ripped open.

She makes me hurt.

She makes me bleed like no one else.

Yet she is the only thing that can heal the wounds and staunch the bleeding.

I push off from the counter, swiping the bottle of whiskey that I took from Roxy and leave. I don't make it to the stairs though. My body pulls me in another direction, and I find myself standing over Roxanne as she sleeps.

"Watching someone sleep is a new level of creepy, Maddox," Roxanne mumbles sleepily.

"Just another thing to add to my extensive repertoire of fucked up shit I'm good at."

She scoffs, snuggling down further into her pillow. "I'm not sure bragging is appropriate for your level of crazy."

I crouch in front of her. "Not all my talents are bad, you know?"

One eye opens, and she cocks a sceptical brow. "I'm not sure the ability to be an arsehole counts as a good talent, Maddox. But I'll give you points for trying."

"Oh, Roxanne, you haven't even scraped the surface of my arseholishness yet." I lean forward, unable to stop myself, and plant a kiss on her forehead. It's soft and gentle—two things that are never used in the same sentence when it comes to describing me. I hold there a moment longer than needed, but her smell and the taste of her is addicting. It seems I'm not the only one affected. Her head lifts slowly, forcing my lips further down her face until they are met with hers. The scent of cherries fires a shot of desire straight to my dick. I've been fucking hard for days.

I've been hard for Roxanne all my fucking life.

Her lips part, allowing me in, and I don't waste a damn second of the invitation. I grip her head, wrapping my fingers in her hair as hers tangle in my t-shirt. I can almost hear the tear of fabric her grasp is so tight.

I drop my arse to the floor, pulling her with me. Breaking the kiss on a harsh breath, she slides from the sofa, straddling me, and takes my mouth again.

The only thing between the wet heat of her pussy and my raging cock are her knickers, which are damp with her own juices, and my jeans.

Our tongues dual as she grinds against me, and I swallow every one of her whimpers as the friction burns between us.

Releasing her head, my hands wrap around her thighs, fingers digging into her flesh in a bruising grip, and I lift her and climb to my feet before carrying her upstairs.

At the top, I slam her against the wall, needing more from her. Needing to feel her skin. With her pinned in place, I tear her t-shirt from her body and drop my head, taking in a nipple. Sucking and biting and grazing my teeth across the sensitive flesh while she squirms against me. Her legs tighten round me, and she uses the wall as leverage, curling her hips along my hard length.

"O-oh fuck! Maddox..." Her words trail off as I bite down hard on her nipple before letting go. Pulling her away from the wall, her hands grasp my face as my fingers dig impossibly deeper into the cheeks of her arse.

"I need..." she pants out, unable to finish as my fingers slip beneath the lace trim of her knickers and glide effortlessly through her slick folds.

"I've got you, Tinks. I've fucking got you." I ram two fingers into her weeping, swollen pussy, and she jolts in my arms.

I reach my door, pausing against it to pump in and out of her and swallowing her throaty moans with my mouth as her orgasm builds.

I ease up, stalling her orgasm and fumble with the door just as the sound of another door opening reaches me.

Stepping inside my room, I leave the door wide open and stride to my bed as my fingers begin to weave their fucking magic inside her pussy again.

Chapter Twenty-Five

Roxy

Maddox drops to sit on his bed, his fingers continuing their punishing assault on my pussy. I'm so damn close, and I've lost all sense of anything except coming apart.

Maddox suddenly pulls out of me, and I almost rip his head off.

"Don't. You. Dare. Stop, Maddox," I grit out between clenched teeth, taking a grip of his hair and yanking his face to mine.

He smirks at my desperation, and part of me hates I'm showing him how much I want this, but she's in the minority on this one. My greedy pussy only has one thing on her mind. Using the moment to move, I unwrap my legs from around him and instead straddle his hips, my feet hanging over the edge of the bed.

"I need to fucking come, Maddox, but"—I trail a hand down my body to my clit, circling it a couple of times—"if you're not up to the job…"

He slaps my hand aside. "Fuck that! Your orgasms are fucking mine, Tinks." My pussy convulses, and I almost come from his words alone, so when he plunges two fingers back inside me, applying pressure to my clit with his thumb, I'm teetering on the edge in a second.

I ride his hand, gripping his shoulders, nails imbedded in his flesh, and chase my climax.

"That's it, Tinks, ride my fucking fingers. Then you're going to ride my fucking cock."

His lips wrap around my nipple, flicking his tongue back and forth before a stinging bite ricochets like a fucking bullet down my body, hitting my clit as I shatter.

"Oh...my...god," I pant breathlessly, and as I come down my movements slow. But I don't get a full breath before Maddox is lifting my hips and ripping open his jeans. I watch as he pulls his cock free, fingers glistening with my orgasm wrap around it as he moves my underwear aside and positions it at my entrance.

I sink slowly down on his shaft, savouring every inch. Impatient, Maddox thrusts upward, hitting my cervix, and seating himself fully inside me.

"Arrrghhhh!" I cry, and catching my breath, I start up a slow pace as I adjust to his size. I dip my head, nipping Maddox's bottom lip before sealing my lips over his and dipping my tongue in and out, mirroring my own movements.

Maddox grunts as he thrusts up, meeting every one of my own. As I breakaway from the kiss, needing to catch a breath, I see Maddox's eyes flick behind me.

The atmosphere in the room intensifies, and every hair on my body stands on end as electricity zips over me.

"Oh shit," I mutter under my breath, and a deep rumbling chuckle comes from Maddox as our rhythm stutters slightly.

A bang comes from behind me as the door is pushed closed. Maddox's fingers find my chin, and he makes sure my eyes are on him before he speaks.

"Get out of your head, Tinks. Don't think, just feel."

A hand tangles in my hair, and Maddox releases my chin as

Zak pulls my head back, arching my back and forcing Maddox deeper inside me. I groan as my clit brushes his pelvic bone, and I hold back the need to do it again.

"Turn around, Rox," he whispers in my ear and lands a sharp slap to my arse. The sting coils low in my belly before unwinding and flooding my veins with pleasure.

The grip on my hair loosens, and I look back to Maddox, who gives a nod. I rise and climb from him on shaky legs. He grips my hips and steadies me before I turn around.

Raising my head, my eyes meet swirling blues that mirror my own, and I watch as they rake over my body, leaving a trail of fire wherever they touch.

Maddox's hands on my hips squeeze, tensing, before moving to caress my arse cheeks, slipping between my thighs and dipping in and out of my pussy.

Zak reaches his own hands out, snagging the flimsy strap of my lace knickers and running his fingers inside.

"You won't be needing these anymore, Rox," he growls, his tone husky and laced with hunger. He rolls them down over my hips then down my legs, crouching as he reaches my feet. I step out of them, and as soon as they are free, Zak is back in front of me.

Maddox's hands pull at my hips again, and I have to step back so as not to stumble. As I get closer to him, he lifts me.

"Feet on the edge of the bed, Rox," Zak demands roughly, as I'm lifted in the air, and I place a foot either side of Maddox's thighs.

Maddox lies back, and I rest a hand behind me to balance, while I use the other to line his cock up with my entrance. This time, I don't wait, I slam myself down on him.

"Fuck!" Maddox hisses.

Maddox wraps his arms beneath my thighs to hold me up then begins thrusting into me, and I watch Zak the whole time. He's shirtless, and sweat glistens on his body already, so I assume he was working out before he came in here. The outline of his cock is clearly visible through his grey joggers, and knowing I'm watching him, he runs a hand over it before giving it squeeze.

Oh fuck!

Zak drops his joggers to the floor as I feel the whispers of another orgasm building, and he follows them, dropping to his knees between my spread legs, and oh my fucking god, he's...

Zak leans forward, flicking his tongue over my clit. He looks up at me through hooded eyes, which spark devilishly, as he dives back in. This time, he doesn't stop.

My body floods with sensations that are overwhelming, but I don't stop them. I can't fucking stop them. Every inch of my skin is alive, and every touch, every thrust is like a tiny firework exploding inside me.

Heat spreads like wildfire as the walls of my pussy clamp down on Maddox, and I almost lose my footing. Zak's hands lock behind my knees, holding me in place as I ride his face with each thrust of Maddox's cock.

The room fills with grunts and groans, and my whimpers become a never-ending string of prayers that turn to a choked cry as I hurtle off the precipice into another orgasm.

Zak's eyes meet mine, and he makes one last slow lick, flattening his tongue, before pulling away. Maddox's thrusts slow, and I'm confused for a moment knowing he's not done.

My legs are lowered to the ground at the same time Zak rises to his feet, a hand fisting his cock. An arm wraps around my waist as Maddox sits up and lifts me off him. I raise my head just as Zak swipes the back of his hand across his chin, wiping the evidence of my last climax away.

He steps forward, leaning down and taking my mouth, stealing all the breath from me. When he pulls back, Maddox spins me to face the bed, and with a slap to my arse, he urges me up onto it.

The space in my head where my brain used to be is filled with a blissed-out fuzz, and I climb up onto all fours as Zak walks around and does the same, kneeling in front of me.

My mouth waters as Zak's hand pumps his shaft, precum glistening on the tip, and my tongue runs the length of my bottom lip as I feel Maddox behind me, tormenting me with the head of his cock against my entrance.

Stretching my body forward on my elbows, I look up to Zak and make my intentions clear. His eyes sparkle with excitement and eagerness as I stick my tongue out, swirling it around the rim before sucking him into my mouth just as Maddox slams back inside me.

My hum of pleasure is drowned out as Zak fists my hair and thrusts forward, hitting the back of my throat and causing me to gag, which in turn has me clenching around Maddox's cock as he thrusts in and out of me.

It doesn't take long for that heat to warm in my lower belly again as Maddox and Zak synchronise their movements, speeding up as they reach the peak of their pleasure. Maddox breaks first, coming with a rapturous roar that could wake the dead.

At the first note of Maddox's echoing cry, Zak swells, ridge scraping against my teeth, as he shoots his cum to the back of my throat, and I swallow it all as my own orgasm hits.

Zak withdraws from my mouth, and I take hold of him, licking him clean before collapsing in an exhausted heap on the bed. Maddox drops down beside me on one side and Zak on the other.

My eyes heavy and body sore and sated, I drift off to sleep cocooned by two men who I haven't slept like this with since we were kids, and who I always believed would never hurt me.

I wake to an inferno of heat surrounding me and a buzzing noise. The buzzing stops, and I let my eyes drift closed again. As soon as they shut, the damn buzzing starts again.

"Damn it!" I mumble, as I attempt to extricate myself from between Maddox and Zak. An arm winds its way round my stomach.

"Where do you think you're going?" Comes a deep husky growl as I'm pulled back into tattooed arms. A trail of kisses is placed along my shoulder up to my neck as a hand cups my breast, tweaking my nipple between firm fingers. I close my eyes and lose myself to the pleasure for a second, all thought of the buzzing noise forgotten. My greedy vagina is totally on board with what Zak's offering this morning. I lift my leg, allowing his rock-hard cock to slip between my already soaked folds.

He rocks back and forth as few times, brushing the head over my clit, and I can't hold back the little moan as he stops at my entrance, nudging in just a little at a time. It's painfully torturous but equally delicious.

He slides the rest of the way in, and my eyes snap open as I let out a full-on groan. Honey-hazel-coloured eyes stare back at me, and the corner of his mouth is kicked up.

"Good fucking morning, Tinks. What a way to wake up," he drawls, then he leans forward and takes a nipple into his mouth as Zak begins to move behind me.

"Oh fuck!" I hiss, but I'm cut short a second later as a loud bang comes from downstairs, and then voices can be heard in the hallway. Very loud and very distinctive voices. My groans of pleasure are suddenly turned to exclamations of "oh shit".

Reluctantly, we scramble from the bed and attempt to dress, which is a little difficult for me as I've no clothes in here. Maddox throws me a t-shirt, and I pull it over my head quickly and make for the door only to be yanked back. Lips land on mine, possessive and demanding, but they're gone as quick as they came.

"We'll finish this later." Is all Maddox says before disappearing out the door and leaving me standing there.

"Hey," Zak says behind me, and I turn to him. He doesn't get another word out before a female voice hollers from downstairs.

"Roxy! Roxy! Where are you?"

"Fuck! I need to get down there before World War 3 breaks out." I try to turn, but Zak stops me, spinning me back round, and doing the same as Maddox, hands gripping my face as his lips meet mine. His kiss is as possessive as Maddox's, but there's a tenderness there too. He lets me go, and I feel a little lightheaded before catching my breath. Zak lands a slap to my arse as I exit the room and hurry to my room and pull on some underwear and joggers.

Descending the stairs, the voices have risen a level, and I stop at the bottom and take in the scene before me. Rick is holding back Jess as she shouts and points her finger at Maddox, who stands with his arms folded across his chest and a blank, unaffected look on his face.

Rick, however, looks like he's about ready to commit murder, and I'm not sure if it shouldn't be Jess holding him back.

Jess' eyes land on me, and her angry rant comes to a halt. Rick releases her, and she shoves past Maddox to reach me, wrapping me in a hug.

"I can totally murder him, right?" she whispers.

I shake my head and chuckle as I pull away. "He has his uses," I jest, pinning my gaze on Maddox, who has now turned to watch Jess and me. Letting me go, I move toward Rick, who pulls me in for a hug too and drops a kiss on my cheek.

Two deep, synchronised growls come from behind us, and I feel a rumble of laughter in Rick's chest.

"I don't like them, Roxy, but I appreciate their caveman mentality." He doesn't even attempt to keep his words between us. I step back out of his arms, casting a quick glance over my shoulder at Maddox and Zak. The look on their faces is quite possibly the deadliest I've seen so far, and a flutter of... something winds its way through my belly.

Turning back, my eyes land on a third person, and someone I've not met before. Rick sees where my gaze is and turns to introduce us.

"Drew, meet Roxy," Rick says, as Drew reaches out a hand for me to shake. "And Maddox and Zak Lawler," he continues, pointing to each of the guys in turn. There're no handshakes offered with their introductions, just a simple nod in acceptance they've heard who each of them is and written their names down for future reference if needed.

There's an awkward moment of silence before I say, "Shall we." And I direct Rick, Jess and Drew to the lounge.

There's a grunt from Maddox as the three of them trail past into the lounge, and I turn to him with a look of warning.

"Knock it off," I tell him.

"I'll knock *him* off if he touches you like that again," Maddox mumbles as I enter the lounge behind the others.

Once everyone is settled, I explain to Rick what I need, even though Jess has no doubt already told him.

"What's the rest of the story, Roxy? 'Cause if you think I'm putting Jess' and Max's life in danger without knowing the full story, you're sorely mistaken," Rick tells me, and I watch as Jess runs a hand over his thigh, giving a shake of her head when he looks at her.

"Jess, it's fine. I wouldn't expect anything less from him, but unfortunately, it's not my story to tell," I say, looking to

Maddox and Zak where they sit on the opposite side of the room.

After a minute, Maddox says, "What do you want to know?"

Rick pins him with a hardened stare. "If you want me to keep them safe then I need to know everything. Nothing left out. I want to know who's likely to be looking for them and why."

"Well then, I guess this was pointless. I'm not telling you fuck all. If I had my way Axel would be dead and buried for what he did."

There's a gasp from the doorway, and all eyes turn in that direction.

"Eva," I say, rising to my feet. Her eyes jump between us all as I make my way to her slowly. "It's okay. These are my friends, and I'm hoping they are going to get you out of London to somewhere safe for a while."

"And what about Axel, huh?" Her eyes fill with unshed tears, but she doesn't let them fall. Instead, she turns to Maddox. "Do you have any idea how difficult this has been for him? Betraying the only two people who've ever given a damn about him. It's been eating him up inside. How you can stand there and talk about killing him like he's nothing makes me sick. You're just like my fath—"

Maddox is on his feet in a second, cutting of the rest of Eva's words, and Zak snatches hold of him. Drew, who is standing closest to the door, moves to Eva's side. I raise a curious brow at his eagerness to protect her having only known her for less than a minute.

"Okay, enough. Jess, how about you, me and Eva go get something to drink in the kitchen. I spin Eva toward the door, who is shaking and wide eyed, as Jess takes the other side of her, and we lead her out to the kitchen.

Settling her on a chair at the dining table, I make us some

tea, then join Eva and Jess.

"Look, Eva, you need to understand something—"

"I understand just fucking fine. Maddox and Zak are just like the rest of these arseholes that think they own the streets. Kill or be killed, right? But you know what? I don't want this life. I don't want this for our child". Her hand automatically rubs her small bump. "My mother died making sure my bastard father never discovered I exist. I should never have stayed here in London."

Jess lifts her cup, taking a sip, before saying, "Do you mind me asking why you did then?"

Eva seems thrown by the question for a moment, as though she expected a different question, and I hold my breath knowing what's coming. "I...had a sister, younger than me. She went missing just after my mum was murdered."

Nausea roils in my gut, and I daren't look at Jess. Give her her due, she doesn't take her eyes from Eva or show any reaction to what Eva just said.

Eva continues, "I wanted to find her." Her eyes glass over again at the memory.

Jess casts a quick glance my way, and I give her a nod. "Did you?"

"No," she says with a deep sorrow that only someone whose ever had a loved one go missing could understand.

"Come on, I'll take you to see Axel." Her eyes brighten instantly, and she jumps to her feet. I walk to the door leading to the cellar but turn before opening it. "Eva, he's..."

"Just take me to him. Please," she pleads.

I lead her down the stairs, opening the door and stepping aside so she can enter first. I watch from the door as she lays her eyes on him all battered and bruised.

The relief evident on his face when he looks up and sees her standing there causes my heart to skip several beats. She rushes to his side, dropping down to her knees as she reaches the bed. She hesitates, not wanting to hurt him, before running gentle fingers over the cuts to his face.

I turn away, not wanting to intrude on their private moment, and find Jess looking at me.

"I get it, Rox, I really do, but are you sure about this?"

"Yes, JJ, I'm sure. I know I'm asking a lot and possibly putting you at risk, but I don't know what else to do."

She looks over my shoulder to where Axel and Eva are huddled together and talking quietly. "Does she know? Do they?" she asks, pointing a finger to the ceiling.

"Why I want to help her, no. About Star, yes. It's part of the reason why I agreed to this shit in the first fucking place. But Eva knows nothing other than I'm a corrupt cop."

Jess opens her mouth to respond, but she's cut short when we hear footsteps coming down the stairs a split second before my name is called out.

"Rox?"

"We'll talk later," I whisper just as Zak comes in to view. "Hey, what's up?" I ask as he reaches us, plastering a smile on my face.

His eyes scan the scene behind me before coming back to me. "Rick wants to talk to Eva and Axel."

"That's good, right?" I ask Jess.

"It's a step in the right direction. And you and I are going to talk before I leave, Rox," she says, then heads for the stairs.

Zak steps into me, forcing me back a step. "What is it you two need to talk about, exactly?" His voice is gravelly and sends a shiver of arousal the length of my body, which is still a little buzzed from earlier.

"Girl talk, nothing for you to worry about," I reply, attempting to sound casual, but it comes out somewhat breathy. The small bar in his brow catches in the light as he arches it with a look that calls me out as a liar. I hold his gaze despite the building need to look away from his intense eyes.

"I would suggest that you can tell me all about it later, but I have a very strong feeling your mouth is going to be busy doing other things."

Oh fuck! I need to get some distance between us.

Thankfully, we are interrupted as Eva and Axel approach, and Zak takes a step away from me and looks to Axel. He's still looking worse for wear but healthier than he has since I first saw him.

Axel gives me a nod, his arm wrapped around Eva. "Thank you, Roxanne." Genuine gratitude is just visible beneath his bruised faced.

"It's Roxy. Only my mother and one other person calls me Roxanne. And don't thank me yet. My friend would like a chat with you before you can leave." I step aside, allowing them to go first.

I follow behind and can feel Zak on my heels, and when he runs a hand up and over my arse, I spin and give him a reprimanding scowl as I jump up a couple of steps to escape.

My mind is about ready to burst. I've barely had time to pee, let alone process what happened last night, and almost again this morning. The question of 'what the fuck am I doing?' is like a battering ram inside my head right now.

I veer off as we near the lounge door, telling Zak I need the toilet when he stops me to ask where I'm going. Again, he looks unconvinced with my answer, and I can't blame him. I don't need the toilet at all. What I need is a fucking minute to gather my thoughts. Being in a room with both Maddox and Zak is how I imagine lab rats feel under observation. Every move I make, everything I say is all absorbed and scrutinised down to the ninth degree. It makes me want to run away.

But I'm Roxy Whitmore, and I've never ran away from anything in my life.

I sure as fuck don't intend to start now.

Chapter Twenty-Six

Zak

R ox isn't fooling me at all with her bullshit disappearing act or her 'girl talk' comment down in the cellar. I heard way more than she thinks I did.

Maddox and I have been doing our own investigation into what happened to Star, but now it seems that Rox knows more than we do. And by the sound of it, Eva is connected in some way or other.

Entering the lounge, Axel and Eva are just taking a seat, introductions obviously over, and Rick is wearing a disapproved frown, which he's throwing in the direction of Maddox. No doubt at the state of Axel's face. It's a good job he can't see the rest of his body.

Maddox, however, isn't in the slightest bothered by the eyes burning a hole in the side of his face, he's too busy looking at me. His eyes asking the question of where Rox is. I raise my chin to him to let him know she's coming. I'm not sure if that's a lie or not.

Tuning into the conversation going on between Axel and Rick, I hear Rick asking questions about possible threats. He demands answers in a commanding tone that only an ex-military man can.

After a couple of minutes, Rick now having turned his questions to Eva, Maddox comes and stands beside me. Keeping close eyes on Rick and this Drew guy that tagged along with him, he whispers, "Where is she?"

"Bathroom break. Give her a minute," I reply. And as if she heard us talking about her, she strolls in. Her back is straight, her chin held high and her fierce look of composure back in place.

My dick perks up, and I curse beneath my breath at its shitty timing. Images of her riding Maddox while I eat her out invade my mind and don't help one fucking bit. Made even worst as she strolls past us, and I get a heady waft of her perfume.

Rox takes up position next to Jess, standing behind the sofa that Rick is seated on as he continues to grill Axel and Eva.

"Is there anything else you can tell me about Laskin, Eva? Anything at all." She shakes her head but keeps her eyes down.

It's a lie.

Rick keeps his gaze on her, letting her know he's not falling for it either, but a minute later, he turns to us.

"Bonner and Rogers, what's—"

"You don't need to worry about them," Maddox states defensively.

Rick chuckles. "Okay, big man, I call bullshit on that." I feel Maddox tense beside me, and I even catch Rox wince. "If Whitmore is here, in whatever this fucked up mess you've involved her in, then I want more than 'you don't need to worry about them' as a guarantee."

"I don't owe you a damn thing, least of all an explanation about *my* business, *Sergeant Sullivan*," Maddox fires back.

Rick rises to his feet. "If you want my help, then you

better start talking. And it's Lieutenant Sullivan, you piece of shit."

Maddox is so fucking fast when he moves, I almost miss latching onto his arm, but I do just as Drew steps in between Rick and Maddox. Jess comes to Rick's side, and Rox pushes her way past Drew to stop in front of Maddox.

Fury flashes in her eyes and her nostrils flare. "Out!" she orders, but Maddox hasn't even looked at her yet. Smacking his chest to get his attention, she tells him again, "Out now, Maddox. I've had enough of this bollocks. Fucking men and their ridiculous 'I've got a bigger dick than you' bull crap."

Finally, his gaze drops to her, and I already know what's going through his mind. God help Rox.

His only response is a growl before he steps back, and I can see that Rox thinks she's won. Fool. Her posture relaxes a little just as Maddox strikes. Swiping her off the floor and over his shoulder, he turns and strides from the room to a chorus of 'what the fuck are you doing?' and 'put me the fuck down!'

I shake my head, turning back to the room and the shocked faces of everyone. The only person who looks remotely amused is Jess. I like her. And despite the fact he rubs Maddox up the wrong way, I actually like Rick.

Maddox and he share a lot of similar traits, least of all being an overbearing cunt. Maria comes into the lounge halting further questions or commotion and carrying a tray of pastries. She doesn't bat an eye at the continuing shouts coming from Rox and places the tray on the coffee table.

"Please help yourselves. Can I get anyone a drink? Tea, coffee, beer?"

I feel eyes on me and turn to see Axel watching me. I give him a nod to let him know that we are good, and he returns it before grabbing a croissant for Eva and one for himself.

I'm about to sneak off when a voice from behind stops me.

"Have fun." Twisting my head, I see Jess striding toward me while taking a bite of an almond twist.

"Excuse me?" It's a stupid question. I know exactly what she meant.

"Pretend all you like, but I see the way you look at her, both of you." She tilts her head, a smirk pulling at her mouth. "Be warned, Zak, don't fucking hurt her," she says casually, a grin still on her face.

I don't show any reaction to her threat, and it's not because I don't think she means it. On the contrary, Jess isn't one to make idol threats. She doesn't realise we know about her past and the part Rox played in helping Jess get revenge on the guys that hurt her as a teen. Something else we have our little friend to thank for that.

"Duly noted. Now, if you'll excuse me, I have somewhere else I need to be. Make yourself at home, Jess." I walk away with a smile on my face.

I jog up the stairs and reach Maddox's door just as a deep groan comes from the other side. My hand rests on the handle, ready to open it and go inside, but something holds me back.

Jess' words have obviously got inside my head more than I thought. I spin on my heels and slip inside my own room, leaving Maddox and Rox to it. It's not that I don't want to be in there with them. God, I'd love nothing more than to be balls deep inside her again, but I feel Maddox needs her more right now.

I run a hand through my hair as I pace my room feeling agitated, but I can't place where it's stemming from. Something feels off. Something is coming. I have no idea what, but I know we need to be ready.

How the hell do you prepare for something you can't see coming?

Walking to my wardrobe, I open the door, pulling out

trousers and a shirt, but as I'm about to turn away, my eyes snag on a box sitting in the bottom.

Tossing the clothes on the bed, I lean down and lift the box out. Carrying it to the bed, I sit as I flip the lid off. Inside are a stack of photos, many of them taken with an old Polaroid camera, along with several flyers from a couple of raves that Mad and I went to and half a dozen other little mementos from our teen years.

I flick through the photos, most are candid shots of us and Rox pissing around, but a couple of them are posed shots. I stop on one of the three us together. I don't remember who took it, but it looks like we are in Rox's old flat, which she shared with her mum and sister. She's in between us, our arms slung over her shoulders, and a wide and genuine smile lights up her face.

It was taken at a time when things were far less complicated, and we still had a lingering innocence to us. Moving it to the side, the next photo tells of a completely different story. Roving my eyes over the picture, I bring it closer to get a better look at Rox's face as she poses with Maddox's gun. The exact one she was asking about. This time, there's still a smile on her face, but it doesn't reach her eyes, which have a hardened look now. There's no spark at all. I know exactly when this is.

It's the night Theo gifted Maddox the gun. It's the night after Rox had her first run in with Rogers. It's also the night that sealed our fate. We didn't know it then, but it soon became very fucking clear.

A noise in the hallway snaps me from my memories, and I begin putting everything back in the box as Rox's voice filters through to me.

"Not impressed, Maddox."

"I didn't hear you complaining while I was..." His voice trails off as they move further away and head downstairs.

I'm placing the photos back in the box when something

niggles at the back of my mind about them, but I can't put my finger on what. Brushing it off, I shove the lid on the box and put it back in my wardrobe.

Back downstairs, there's no sign of Rox or Jess, and I'm guessing they've gone off to have that 'girl talk' before they all leave with Axel and Eva.

Conversation is stilted in the lounge as Maddox and Rick give each other death glares from across the room, and Maria chats with Eva. Drew stands like a damn sentry at the side of the room.

Axel is sitting next to Eva, but he's not paying attention to their conversation, instead his eyes are on me. He gets to his feet and comes over when our eyes meet.

"Hey, man," he says tentatively. I don't respond above a chin lift, and he takes that as a sign to continue with whatever it is he feels he needs to say. "Look, I'm sorry, Zak. I know that what I did—"

"What you did should have earned you a one-way ticket to a painful end and a place at the bottom of the Thames as fish food. The fact you're still fucking breathing is thanks to one person, and it ain't me or Maddox, man."

"I know. But I need you to know that I would never have given him more, Zak. I'd never have sold you out completely. I'd have given my life before that happened. You and Maddox have been like a family to me."

I finally turn to look at him. "You don't fucking sell out family, Axel. Ever." He goes to cut me off, but I hold a hand up for him to let me finish. "But I get it. Sometimes even loyalty is pushed aside when it comes to those you love. Hell, Maddox and I have compromised ourselves more times than I can count for the very same reason."

Axel nods his agreement, and I know he knows who I'm talking about. He knows because she's the very reason he and Eva are getting out of here safely.

219

We settle into a comfortable silence and a mutual acceptance that past failings should now be left in the past.

After a short time, Axel moves back to his seat beside Eva, and I watch as her hand slides into his and each ask if the other is okay.

It makes me think of the kind of future I want. The kind of future that Maddox and I always wanted but was never possible before. Now though, that future is within grasp, but there is still a long way to go. A lot that still needs to be disclosed and even more that Rox needs to learn and suffer through before we can get there.

I don't doubt that the hate she's been harbouring for us the past ten years is even remotely close to the hate she's going to have when the full extent of our knowledge and involvement comes to light.

I hate so much of my past, but not enough to regret the things I've done. My only regret is the many years of absence from her life. Given the choice, I'd choose the same fucking path every time.

Maddox shifts from where he was leaning against the far wall and comes to stand beside me.

"Will you relax for fuck's sake. They'll be gone soon," I say, thinking that the stern look on his face is down to Axel and Rick still invading his air space.

"Yeah, not fucking soon enough for me. But it's not that. Rocky messaged to say that there's been an increased cop presence around Rogue and The Scarlet Door. This has that cunt Noah's name all over it."

"You think he's planning to make a move on us?"

"Nah, he's got fuck all. But something is definitely brewing. The quicker we deal with this little problem the better," he says, gesturing toward Axel and Eva. "Everything is too quiet everywhere else, and it's making me tetchy as fuck"

"Have you heard from Kavanagh since your meet?"

"No, and that right there should be enough to set the alarm bells ringing. The guy is looking to make ground here, yet he's not pushing to sell more of his shit to us or anyone for that matter, not that I've heard. What's his fucking play if not that?"

"We always knew going to Kavanagh was a risky move but a necessary one after what happened with the shipments. You still think that it was Rogers' intention to force us into using him?"

"Not sure. If it was, why? He's stopped every attempt at us using a new supplier since we cut him off, so why allow Kavanagh in when it's clear he wants a piece of London for himself."

I think over his words and know he's doing the same. Theo dealt in arms with Kavanagh's father years ago, but only on a small level as the Irish are one family Theo wasn't keen to get in with. They had been close in the past apparently, but a feud had severed most of their ties. It's one of the reasons we were so reluctant. Theo was a shrewd businessman, and if he steered clear, there was a damn good reason for it.

I watch Rick check his watch before letting Axel and Eva know that they need to make a move soon.

"I'll go get Rox and Jess," I tell him, and he gives me an appreciative nod.

Chapter Twenty-Seven

Roxy

My feet disappear from beneath me as I'm hauled over Maddox's shoulder and carried from the room while yelling at him to put me down.

The blood rushes to my head as he climbs the stairs two at a time, bouncing me around.

"Maddox," I yell, but my only reply is a slap on my arse, which sends a tingle of need winding through my fog of anger at him. "Jesus! Put me down for fuck's sake. We have visitors. Stop behaving like a damn caveman."

He grumbles about not giving a fuck who's here and stomps through his open bedroom door, slamming it shut behind him.

He slowly slides me down his body as he comes to a stop in the middle of the room. My hands clasp his face as my feet touch ground again.

"I need to be inside you, right fucking now, Tinks." His lips drop to mine, and I expected the kiss to be harsh and delivered with force, like his demand to fuck me, but it's surprisingly gentle.

As he pulls back, his hands find the waistband of my

joggers, and he shoves them down over my arse before spinning me round and walking me toward the bed. Bending me over, he runs a hand between my legs, which part eagerly. Pushing inside me with two fingers, he pumps them a couple of times before pulling out and circling my clit, then he drags his fingers from front to back, gathering my juices as he goes.

When he presses against my puckered hole, I hold back a groan, but I can't stop myself from pushing back against his finger, telling him exactly how much I like it.

"Hmmmm, you like that, Tinks, huh? Good. Because real soon, I'm going to have this arse while Zak fucks that pretty fucking pussy of yours"—his finger slips past my tight ring—"you'll be so fucking full..." He groans as the head of his cock jerks at my entrance, sliding in an inch. I push back again, and this time Maddox rams all the way in with a grunt as his finger slips into my arse all the way to his knuckle.

"I hope you're fucking ready for me, Tinks, 'cause this is going to be hard and fast." He grinds his hips, forcing my withheld groan to break free, and then he devastates me with every thrust, every stroke, until I'm panting through an orgasm that obliterates my mind and body.

I'm a boneless mess as Maddox flips me over, yanking my joggers off before ramming into me as my breath catches and his hand locks around my throat. I watch him through hooded eyes as he hammers his hips, only his grip on my throat prevents me from moving further up the bed on every thrust.

I feel the tell-tale sign of a second orgasm building as Maddox's cock swells, the head rubbing against my tightening walls. My toes curl, legs squeezing Maddox's waist, and fingers gripping the duvet as my climax rushes over me and causing Maddox to do the same. He falls over me, breathing heavily as he buries his head into my neck.

"Fuck me dead. How have I survived this long without

being inside you," he whispers, peppering intimate kisses along my neck between breaths.

The words float through my mind, but it's currently just as fucked as I am and can't make sense of it all.

Maddox's lips capture mine, his tongue a teasing caress before he pulls away, rising on his arms to look at me.

His gaze is penetrating and intense, and if I looked a little deeper, I could read a thousand words in his eyes. But I don't. I can't. Instead, I give a little tap to his sweat slicked chest, telling him to move and he does.

As he tucks himself away, I lift myself from the bed to a sitting position, giving my body a second to recalibrate before climbing to my feet.

My legs are a little jelly like, but I manage to look steady as I seek out my joggers and drag them up my legs when I find them.

I make a move to the door, catching my reflection in the mirrored wardrobe door. Stepping closer, I trace my fingers over the marks on my neck.

Maddox steps up behind me, his hands splaying across my abdomen.

"I like my marks on you, Tinks," he says, dropping his lips to my neck.

I can't breathe as his possessiveness breaks through my muddled thoughts. Pushing out of his arms and away from him, I carry on my way to the door, swinging it open as he steps out behind me.

"Not impressed, Maddox."

"I didn't hear you complaining while I was fucking you, Roxanne." It's a gruff reply, and his use of my real name clues me into the fact he's not happy with my response.

Downstairs, I veer off toward the kitchen, not in the least bit interested in the Maddox and Rox just fucked show. Thankfully, Maddox doesn't try to stop me or follow.

I've barely had a second before Jess breezes into the room, coming straight for me and wrapping me up in a hug. I collapse into her arms as everything over the last few weeks crashes into me.

"Hey, what's going on?" she says, holding my head in her hands and lifting it till I'm looking at her.

"I-I don't know, JJ. Everything is such a fucking mess right now." This is not me. I can't let it be me. I suck in a deep breath as Jess drops her hands from my face.

"This is not the face of someone who just had a hot as fuck ménage, Rox."

"Wh— Aah, fucking hell. That did not happen." She tilts her head at me and raises her brows. "Okay, that did not happen just now."

"Ooh, so it did happen then," she says with a wink. Seeing the look on my face, she changes tac. "Come on, let's sit. What's going on?"

"Where the fuck do you want me to start?" Jess moves around the kitchen, opening cupboards and looking for something. I'm just about to tell her where the strong stuff is when she finds it. Not bothering with glasses, she places the bottle on the table before taking a seat.

"You can start with how you're feeling?"

"Like a rung-out rag, JJ." I pause, and she waits for me to continue. "Rogers put a target on me according to Maddox and Zak."

"Is this because of what happened?" I shrug. "Has to be, but why wait so long, and what the hell does this have to do with the guys?"

"That I can answer. They told me that Rogers murdered Theo and is trying to frame them for it. Taking out Theo is twofold, by my thinking anyway. With Theo out the way, Rogers was free to take up the head of the family role, but the Lawlers pose the biggest threat, so—"

"Getting rid of them eliminates the biggest threat to his position."

"Exactly."

"What about Eva, you think what happened to Eva's mum and her sister is connected to Star?"

"I'm almost certain. I've looked at the case files on Eva's mum's death and the similarities are glaringly obvious. I just can't find the fucking connection. I know I could have asked her, but I don't want to cause false hope. If I find anything out about her sister, then I'll tell her."

"Okay, makes sense. Have they given you anything on what happened to your mum or sister?" I shake my head. "Do you think they know anything or just used it to force you into helping?" She shakes her own head, and before I can reply, she answers her own question. "No, they do. I'm just not sure why they are keeping it from you."

I take the bottle from the middle of the table, tilting it to look at the label and realising it's some sort of Vodka I've never heard of. Unscrewing the cap, I take a deep pull of it before passing it to JJ.

She takes a swig and then looks at me, a serious look on her face. "Do you love them?"

"As much as I hate them," I say immediately. I don't need to think about it because as much as my feelings are messed the fuck up that is something that's never changed. I've always loved Maddox and Zak. But their betrayal turned a big part of that to a hate that's so twisted I don't even know where to begin to unravel it. "But how the fuck am I supposed to trust them again—trust my heart, JJ?"

We pass the bottle between us again, swigging heartily, me more than her. "Yeah, that is a problem I don't envy you for. But if you love them, do you not owe it to yourself to at least try?"

I scoff at her response. "Try as in what exactly? A relationship with two guys is already out there enough, but throw in the fact they are basically brothers, who betrayed and hurt me more than anyone else ever has, and a part of the criminal world I've been locking up for most of my life and you have yourself a recipe for disaster."

"A beautiful disaster though, right?" The corner of her mouth kicks up in a grin. "It was good wasn't it? Tell me it was good," she pleads, leaning forward and waiting for the all the deets.

I try to hold a straight face for as long as possible, but I just can't do it. No matter how I feel or the consequences of what happened between the three of us last night, I can't deny how fucking amazing it was. How much it felt right. How much it felt like a missing piece of me returned home.

"It was good," I say casually with a shrug, but JJ isn't fooled by my fake indifference. I'm saved by footsteps echoing down the hall and heading this way. I take another large mouthful of the vodka before replacing the cap just as Zak appears in the doorway.

"Jess, it's time to go." She gives him a nod and gets to her feet. Zak's eyes rove over me, then to the half empty bottle sitting in the middle of the table, and his brows knit together and his jaw pops in concern.

As Jess heads out, I go to follow, but Zak catches my arm.

"What's going on?" he asks, just as Jess turns back to us.

"I'm coming," I tell her, and she continues on her way. "I told you earlier, girl talk, Zak. I need to go and say goodbye, so..." I look down at where his fingers are loosely wrapped around my bicep.

"Stop lying, Rox. Tell me what's going on in that head of yours."

"Don't fucking talk to me about lying, Zak. You and Maddox have a fucking master's degree in it." The vodka is making it easier to say what I really feel. "I'll stop lying when you start telling me the truth and not this half-cocked version of it that you've been spinning me since you dropped into my life like a heat seeking missile and blew up my world." Damn, that felt good. I yank my arm free and hurry down the hall hoping that an audience will keep anymore confrontations at bay until Rick and Jess have left.

There's a palpable tension among the three us of as I say my goodbyes.

Axel tries to shake my hand, but I brush his hand aside and hug him, careful not to hurt his ribs, several of which are almost certainly broken. I don't miss the uncomfortable look that passes between him and Maddox as I embrace him and tell him to take care.

"Thank you. Be careful, Rox. There's a lot you don't know," he whispers, but as I go to ask what he means, Zak pulls him away from me, giving him a warning glare.

Eva looks extremely uncomfortable and tenses when I hug her. She has absolutely no idea that we share a tragic past baring the same marks. Or how much both our childhoods were spent being hidden from men who wouldn't think twice about harming us or using us to get what they wanted.

"I don't understand why you're helping us?" Eva admits as I let her go.

"I know you don't. Just know that I have my reasons, and one day I hope to be able to share them with you." She accepts my answer, if somewhat a little reluctantly. Questions swim in her eyes, but she remains quiet.

Fire lights my body as I feel Maddox and Zak watching me, no doubt with questions of their own, but ignore them.

There are no growls this time when I hug Rick goodbye, thanking him and squeezing him tight, but then the folded arms and standoffish stance of both Maddox and Zak is more than enough to voice their feelings on the matter.

When JJ steps up to me, I feel tears sting the back of my eyes, but she shakes her head.

"Don't you bloody dare, Rox." She closes her arms around my neck, and we hug like only two best friends can. It's full of everything we want to say but haven't and it's meant to see you through till the next time.

"Be strong, Rox. Don't let your heart or your head rule the other, just trust your instincts. Feel what's right. And do not avoid calling me if you need me. I'll be back here with a damn army in a second if I need to be." Her words almost force those damn tears to spill over, but I hold them in. "You've got this. Love you, girl."

"Love you too, JJ." When she steps back, she hustles out the door without looking back. Cheeky cow telling me not to cry when she's clearly bawling like a baby.

She finally turns to wave as the car pulls away up the drive, and waving back, I watch until the car is out of sight before moving back inside.

Of course, there's a welcoming committee waiting for me when I do.

The vodka that JJ and I drank has had plenty of time to fill my veins with fire, and the fresh air has only helped it along.

"We aren't doing this now or maybe even ever because you, neither of you, have any right to ask or know anything about the past ten years of my life. When you walked away you gave up that right." I push between the wall of muscle attempting to block my escape, and I'm surprised when they let me. But I'm even more surprised when they don't follow me.

Back in the kitchen, I suddenly remember Zak's words from their office at The Scarlett Door and how they know every man I've ever been with. Surely that was just talk. But something tells me it wasn't. My blood runs cold at the thought that all this time, all those years, while I was breaking apart, they've been keeping tabs on me. Why, why, why the fuck would they do that?

I hadn't had much of a chance to process Zak's lust filled confession last time considering what happened after, but now....

Feeling betrayed all over again, I snatch the bottle of vodka from the table and decide the best way to deal with this monumental nightmare is to get absolutely fucking wasted.

I make it back to my room without bumping into anyone, not even Maria. Quietly closing the door, I climb on to the bed and begin to numb myself with the gratefully appreciated assistance of my new friend, vodka.

I've made quite a dent in the second half of the bottle and feel adequately buzzed when I decide to have a makeover. Nothing cheers you up more than reinventing yourself, right.

Pulling out the severely lacking amount of clothes that I own, thanks to whatever bastard set fire to my house, I discover a white vest top with an anarchy symbol emblazoned on the front in red, which perfectly suits my mood right now, and a pair of black combat trousers, fuck knows why I bought them, they're not my usual style at all.

I strip down and throw on the vest top and trousers, but I roll the legs up to my knees, and I even put socks and pumps on. I check my reflection in the floor standing mirror in the corner of my room, smiling at my creativity. As I stand there checking myself out, I realise why the clothes are so significant and why they work so well.

This is me ten years ago.

I slump to the floor in front of the mirror and sit for so long that my arse is numb by the time I tune back in and become aware that I desperately need to pee.

Dragging myself from the floor, I meander to the toilet. I'm washing my hands when my stomach growls out a protest at not having anything but a liquid diet today.

On my way out, I grab the bottle of vodka from the bedside table, carrying it loosely in my fingers as I weave my way down the stairs.

I had planned to satisfy my hangry, growling stomach, but voices in the lounge have me turning that way.

Emboldened with vodka and the reincarnated Roxy from ten years ago, I stomp into the lounge.

Maddox spots me first, causing Zak to stop mid-sentence and swivel around in his seat to see what caught his attention.

"Rox, are you okay?" Zak asks, but it's all just a whoosh inside my ears as my stomach rolls over on itself.

"I-I'm—" My words are halted as vomit fills my mouth. I don't see Maddox move, but as my stomach attempts to reject the foul vodka laced sick in my mouth again, a small plastic bin is placed in front of me. I don't—or can't—hold it in any longer and grasp the bin, raising it to my mouth.

After I'm spent, Maddox takes the bin from me, and Zak steers me to the sofa where I collapse down on to it in a heap and close my eyes as I rest my head back.

"Did we miss the memo about a Roxy nineties revival?" Zak jokes, the sofa sinking as he sits beside me.

"Very fucking funny, Zak." A tap to the side of my leg has me cracking an eye open to see Maddox standing over me with a glass of water.

"Drink," he growls, pushing the glass closer to me.

Taking the glass, I raise my head and take a couple of small sips before resting it on my lap.

"Maria is making you some food, and once you've eaten something and sobered up, we're going to talk."

"Wow, if I'd known all I had to do to get you to talk and be honest was take a step back in time, get pissed like we used to at the underpass and then throw up, I wouldn't have waited so long, Maddox," I snipe back. He can't see it, but my eyes roll behind my lids, and it's not from the vodka.

I must have passed out because when I wake the room is dark, except a small sliver of light from the outside lights, which glints off the fireplace. I shift a little, testing the vulnerable state of my stomach. When it appears safe to move, I sit up and realise someone placed a blanket over me as it slips down my body.

"Hello, Sleeping Beauty. Welcome back to the land of the living," drawls a gruff voice from behind me and to the right.

"I must be in the wrong fucking fairy tale. Shouldn't you be riding a white horse and waking me with a kiss?"

"I see your little alcohol induced nap hasn't improved your mood at all. Want to explain how we went from screwing to this?"

"I guess the same way we went from being friends to abandoning me, huh."

"That's not fair, Roxanne."

"Not fucking fair? Are you out of your damn mind? *Fair*, he says." I tut under my breath because I'm honestly speechless.

"You don't know—"

"Don't know what, Maddox? Why I'm back here. Why you left me in the first place. Why the fuck can't I stop letting you and Zak climb inside my body at the drop of a fucking hat when you can't even be honest with me." My voice waivers a little on the last part as emotion takes over. Finding my voice again, I say, "Do you even know? Because I'm starting to think maybe, just maybe, you got a little bored with your life of crime and thought, I know let's screw Roxy over again 'cause it was sooooo much fucking fun the first time round." I get to my feet, suddenly needing out of this room.

"Where are you going?" he demands.

"Well, unless you have that bin handy again and wish to

watch me squatting over it while I take a piss, then I'm going to the toilet." I try not to read too much into the fact he ignored my question as I shuffle from the room.

Once relieved, I go to the kitchen to get a much-needed drink. My mouth is as dry as sandpaper. I fill my glass and think about all the things Maddox and Zak are keeping from me while I drink it down.

I don't understand any of this. I thought chatting to JJ would help me sort it out in my head, but if anything, it's just confused me more. It's probably a good job I'm not a cop anymore. What good am I when I can't even solve my own fucking mystery.

I remember saying that to Mitch after I joined the force and was getting nowhere with solving my sister's disappearance. His words echo in my mind. *'It's not so easy when you're close to it, Rox. You need to step outside the emotion and connection of the case, otherwise it clouds your judgment.'*

The sound of vibrating has me spinning around for the source. The light from a phone on the breakfast bar draws me over. There's no caller ID but the number seems familiar. Snatching it from the top, I swipe to answer and lift it to my ear. Not a word has passed my lips as a male voice hollers down the line.

"Maddox, where's Roxy? She there with you? We have a big fucking problem." My mouth opens and closes like a drowning fish trying to suck in a wisp of oxygen as recognition hits.

I pull the phone away, staring at the screen in abject horror as I hear his voice yelling Maddox's name.

"Maddox! Maddox, did you fucking hear me. The cops are on their way."

Putting it back to my ear, I finally manage to get a word out. Just one. "Mitch?"

"Oh shit," he whispers before the phone is ripped from

me, and I hear Maddox talking to... I can't even. Oh my fucking god.

My knees buckle, and as I drop to the floor, my arm slides across the counter, knocking off my glass. I don't hear it shattering or feel it as a piece flies up nicking my cheek. I don't hear the shouting going on around me or the thump, thump of someone banging on the door. All I can hear is my heart as it splinters into a million pieces again.

"Rox! Rox, hey, you need to listen to me, baby." Zak's face swims in front of me, his hands gripping my shoulders. "It's not what you think, Rox." His hands move to my face as more voices, loud voices, come from down the hall. "Listen to me, we love you. And I need you to trust that. I need you to remember that. Please, Rox."

Hands wrap tightly around my biceps, and I'm hauled to my feet as a man pulls Zak away from me. His hands slip from my face, and my arms are pulled behind my back as cold metal snaps around my wrists. Chaos erupts around me, and I see Maddox being held by two more men as he fights to get away.

A voice to my left finally snaps me out of my daze, and I turn to see Noah.

"Roxanne Whitmore, I'm arresting you on suspicion of the murder of Theo Rogers. You do not have to say anything..."

"Noah?" He doesn't stop or falter as he continues to read me my rights. I hear my name as I'm led from the room.

"Roxanne!" It's a cry of pain and rage and a sound like no other. I stumble as I hear a whoosh of air, and I turn to see Maddox being wrestled to the floor while Zak is being restrained over the kitchen table.

I'm shoved roughly in the back, forcing me to turn around, but I twist my head again as I'm marched outside. I can't see what's going on anymore, and as a car door is opened, a hand on my head pushes me down into the back seat.

At the station, Noah stands beside me like he doesn't even know me as I'm booked in. And I feel sick.

So fucking sick.

The closing of the cell door is a like a bullet to my brain and obliterates everything I am.

To be continued in book 2 Ruthless Vengeance

Thank you for reading!

Are you screaming at your kindle? How much are you hating me right now? I know, cliffhangers suck, but they are a necessary evil. Lol. Thank you for reading, and despite the cliffy, I hope you enjoyed the first part of Roxy's story.

The concluding part of the Retribution Duet is scheduled for release on the May 19th, 2022, and you can pre-order your copy now.

Acknowledgments

There are so many people to thank for making Lawless Deception possible, but the biggest thank you must go to my amazing husband and children for putting up with my long work hours, my constant chatter about plots, characters, graphics and everything else in between. Without their continuous faith and support none of this would be possible.

Thank you to my fantastic Alpha reader, Marnie. You my lady are an absolute godsend. Thank you to my amazing Betas, Megan, Robyn, Julie and Jamie. Your comments and advice are invaluable to me. Love you all hard.

I need to say a special thank you to all my Breachers! You know who you are, and I'm thankful every day that you are in my life. Always there when I need a ridiculous question answered or the metaphorical ledge is too close. Your continuous support and help is very much appreciated, and I may have jumped off the ledge without you all.

Special thanks to Wendy Saunders, who not only takes time out of her own busy schedule to format my books but is always at the end of the phone to offer advice, support and answer a barrage of questions.

A big thanks to my little group of fellow mums for cheering me on and brainstorming with me, resulting in many a side-splitting moment of laughter at our local pub and coffee shop. How we haven't been barred for the content of our conversations is beyond me. Here's to many more.

Huge thanks to Lou at LJ Designs for another stunning

cover and beautiful graphics. You truly are a special lady, and I can't thank you enough for all that you do for me.

A huge thank you to all my ARC readers for reading and to all the bloggers and bookstagrammers for your continued support.

And lastly, but by no means least, a massive thanks to my readers. Without you all none of this would be possible.

About the Author

Imogen Wells is a dark romantic suspense author from the East of England, where she lives with her husband, three children and the family dog and cat.

After being a stay-at-home mum to her three children, Imogen decided to go back to school. Much to her teenage son's amusement. And in 2020 she graduated with a First-Class Honours degree in History and English Literature.

When she is not reading or writing, she loves to binge new shows on Netflix or catch up with old favourites, such as Friends.

Printed in Great Britain
by Amazon